THE SEA KNOWS MY NAME

THE SEA KNOWS MY NAME

LAURA BROOKE ROBSON

Dial Books

Dɪᴀʟ Bᴏᴏᴋs
An imprint of Penguin Random House LLC, New York

First published in the United States of America by Dial Books,
an imprint of Penguin Random House LLC, 2022

Visit us online at penguinrandomhouse.com.

Library of Congress Cataloging-in-Publication Data is available.

Book manufactured in Canada

ISBN 9780525554066

10 9 8 7 6 5 4 3 2 1

FRI

Design by Cerise Steel
Text set in Parango

FOR ALL THE GIRLS WITH STORIES TO TELL

PART ONE

THE MYTH OF CLEMENTINE

THEN AND NOW AND THEN

When my mother was born, her parents named her Clementine, invoking the sweet and unobjectionable, because they forgot that children never live up to their names.

My grandfather was among the first scholars to study genetics, so he was confident in the biological stuff he passed along to his daughter. His wife—harder to be sure of, but she had no obvious deficits. So: a girl. Clementine. Had she been a boy, I'm told they would've named her Rupert, after my grandfather.

Rupert Morgan, a good man: a hobby taxidermist, an outspoken contributor to all the prestigious Astorian academies, and a stalwart proponent of rationality. His wife, a good woman: quiet.

As Clementine grew, it became clear to her parents that she was a mean child, especially to her mother. Clementine didn't have friends, but she did have admirers. My parents met when they were nineteen. My father was studying biology at the university, and he'd heard stories about Professor Rupert Morgan's clever daughter.

As the tale goes, my father went to Rupert's house to plead

his case: He wanted to meet Clementine. Not to take on a date, mind you. But to help him with his research.

Rupert laughed genially and sent him away, but Clementine had overheard. She climbed out her window without a single belonging, shook my father's hand, and said, "But you'll be *my* assistant, yes?"

It hardly matters, at this point, if that's what she actually said. It's part of her myth by now.

Clementine thought my father's studies were interesting, and thought he was interesting too. But the most important thing he gave Clementine was an excuse to leave her parents forever. They hadn't let her enroll in the university; for that, she'd never forgive them.

In time, Clementine would be legend. Not for her science, as she'd once hoped. People would know her name, and people would fear it. No one would remember the sweet and unobjectionable. They would think *pirate* and *queen* and *goddess, harpy* and *bitch* and *snake*. They'd be right, all of them, in time.

I've always thought she started to plan her legacy when my father showed her the Classical myths.

When Clementine was pregnant, bored, and angry, my father brought her facsimiles of the myths from the university library. She read them, I think, and decided she wouldn't settle for being mortal. Wouldn't settle for a story that could be forgotten.

Her obsession was with Libera and Thea, the twin goddesses. Libera, for whom the sea was named, was the goddess of motherhood. So fruitful were her loins that every other god in the myths had a baby with her. Sometimes, Libera even agreed to it.

Her sister, Thea, was the goddess of reason. Being the reasonable sort, she stayed a virgin all her life so no one could cloud her judgment. Upon seeing the atrocities of man, Thea descended onto the world with a spear and thrice stabbed— once in each eye, once in the heart—anyone who did not show her respect.

I was born three weeks premature and silent.

My mother named me Thea.

Chapter One

NOW

Seventeen Years Old

Liberan Sea

I climb to the main deck of the *Pelican* at dawn, expecting it to smell better than the sour, sweaty sleeping quarters packed full of snoring men. It doesn't. It smells like dead whale.

The whale's leviathan, half-stripped body towers in my periphery. *Oh, Thea,* it seems to say, judging. *You stupid, stupid girl. What have you done?*

Too much. Not enough. I'm sorry.

The deck is mostly empty, save the whale's sad body and mine. Besides us, just a few tired sailors shuffle around the sails, trying to coax movement out of the windless dawn. I wrap my hands around the railing and breathe.

I always thought morning horizons were the best part of sailing—a refreshing, a newness—but today doesn't feel fresh or new. Clementine would've told me that admiring the sunrise was sentimental nonsense, and now I see she's right. Yesterday, I ran away from Clementine with a boy I never should've trusted, and I hoped that in dawn, I'd realize it was all a bad dream. But in dawn, all I see is the endless spill of consequence: The morning horizon can't save me.

The sun shakes away the darkness, bayoneting the waves in short-lived colors. Black oil to quicksilver, silver to a urine gold, then the pink-red of diluted wine. In the distance, where an untrained eye would see smudgy nothing, I catch the faintest glimmer of land. I try to be stirred by awe and am not.

"That's the greenhand's girl?" one of the sailors asks behind me.

"Last captain I sailed with didn't let any family on his ship," the other responds loudly. "Said women were bad luck."

"She look sort of familiar to you?"

I turn. The sailors both jolt, just a little, like they're surprised I didn't pretend I couldn't hear them, as any polite woman would know to do.

"I'm not anybody's *girl*," I say.

The first sailor says to the second, "She looks kind of like that pirate—you know the one. The woman."

"A woman pirate?"

"Oh, come off it. How many lady pirates are there? The Fowler one."

"No. The crazy one? Does Captain know that?"

I think of that word, *crazy*, how it would scrape the inside of my dry mouth, how it would lodge there. *Crazy.* Clementine is volatile, decisive, stoic, exacting, irascible, audacious. Contradictory, impossible to please, and so fiercely disappointed in me that when I ran away from her yesterday, I hoped I'd never need to look back.

Is she crazy?

No; she's just what she has to be in a world full of men like these.

"I'm her daughter," I say.

The sailors blink.

"What are you doing on our ship?" one of them asks. "She going to come after us now?"

"Probably not," I say. Not unless she thinks I've been kidnapped; not unless her honor is at stake.

The sailors seem wary of me now that they know I'm the daughter of the cool, the commanding, the crazy Clementine Fowler. But I don't deserve their wariness. I feel weak and small and afraid, lost from my mother, on a ship full of men and one very dead whale.

My heart is beating too fast. I can feel it working away in my chest, *ping ping ping ping ping,* like the heart of the mouse I found in our kitchen when I was ten, so panicked that I thought its eyes might pop out of its head like lids on boiling kettles. I brought the mouse outside and set it in the grass, and it ran so fast I couldn't see where it went. Maybe it shot into a fox's burrow or under a bird's nest. Any danger, it seemed to think, was better than the one it had just experienced in my hands.

If someone set me in a field of tall grass right now, I would run so fast no one could see where I went.

"What's wrong with her?" one of the sailors is saying, waving a hand too close to my face.

I flinch. Then bare my teeth. That's always been the thing separating Clementine and me; for her, the natural reaction is the teeth baring. For me, it's learned, poorly.

"I *said*, how'd you meet the greenhand?"

My future is so, so narrow. I will no longer be Thea. I won't even be Clementine's daughter. I will just be the greenhand's girl, the unnamed possession of an unnamed whaler.

Back on the horizon, the ocean glows faint and flickering under that new sun.

"Where is that?" I ask, ignoring the question, pointing at the smudge of land.

"Providence," one sailor says, because of course it's Providence. "We're not going there. We're docking two settlements south, in Fairshore."

Providence. There should be mountains rising there, but they're obscured by fog.

"How far away?" I ask.

"Fairshore? We should get there tonight."

"No," I say. "Providence."

"Three miles? Why?"

I consider. I consider the smell: rendering blubber; ash; decay. I consider the whale blood in the water, the sharks that come close when they can taste it. I consider the fact that if I stay here, my eyes might pop out of my head like the lids on boiling kettles.

I wrap my fingers around the railing.

Three miles.

No, I can't. That's crazy.

What would Clementine do? the dead whale asks me. *What would Clementine be?*

Volatile, decisive, stoic, exacting, irascible, audacious.

Crazy.

"What are you doing?" one of the sailors asks as I unlace my boots. They're sturdy boots, the kind with good tread that Clementine made all her crew wear. Goodbye, boots. You will be missed. I tug the lace from the left one and use it to tie my hair out of my face.

My jacket, I shrug off. The only thing I take is the knife from the pocket—Clementine's knife, pretty but not delicate, carved with her initials, *CMF*. The gun holster on my hip has been empty since I left Clementine, but I put the knife there now. It's not a perfect fit, but I button it shut and hope it will do.

"*What,*" the sailor says again, louder this time, "are you doing?"

I just want to move. I just want to run. I just want to be.

The railing digs into my knees. I clamber to the top of it. It's slick with water but sticky with salt under my socks, and I sway as I suck in a breath of air.

There you go, the whale says. *One of us should leave this place.*

"Get down from there!" the sailor says, trying to grab my arm, but he's too late, I'm too fast, I'm too free.

I dive.

The water shocks the air from my lungs. Maybe I dove too far. Maybe my body is too heavy, too full of guilt, shame, worry, weakness.

I need air.

Salt in my eyes.

Darkness.

The crown of my head breaks the surface. Then my mouth is free, my neck and the wet hair plastered to it. Air.

When I manage to blink away the salt, I see the hull of the *Pelican* rising from the waves. While I was under, I must've kicked or drifted away—I'm twenty feet from it. But even from this distance, when I'm down here, it's colossal.

The sailors are shouting something blurry and indistinct. Their faces: stunned. Voices: panicked. I did that to them. I am crazy. What a beautiful thing.

I laugh.

"Are you insane?" one of the sailors calls down, cupping his hands around his mouth. "You're going to drown!"

"No," I shout back. "I'm not."

What I don't say—what he doesn't understand—is that drowning is not high on my list of worries right now. It's slid down a few dozen spaces and now ranks below a number of more suffocating fears, like my teakettle skull, or Bauer waking up and smiling at me.

Three miles.

In front of me, the ocean is open, empty, and depthless.

If the sailors call after me for a while, they give up soon enough. If they go tell Bauer I've gone, I'm not worth pursuit.

I am seventeen years old. I am a runaway many times over. I am going to swim.

The water is cold but not too cold. This is the part I try to focus on: the kindness of temperate water. If I focus on this hard enough, I can almost forget that white sharks, which are among the least friendly of the cartilaginous fish, like temperate water too. I can't see anything. The water feels bottomless, and maybe it is—below me, there's a film of dusty green, occasionally interrupted by a tangle of kelp or a drifting cloud of jellyfish. Below that, I imagine barrel-headed sperm whales in water like twilight; stilt-legged spiders in water like midnight; an abyss too black to consider beneath it all.

I swim.

When I think of fear, I think of the barnacles that cling to ships. That's how I imagine my own fear: glued to my skin, visible to all who see me, blemishes to be scraped and carved away. In the ocean, no one can see whether or not I'm afraid. I've never been afraid of water, but this water plays tricks with my head. The endlessness of it. Anything too big to hold in your hands is scary—the depth of the sea, the years of a life, the vastness of human emotion. Usually, my fear comes in breathtaking bursts of panic. Here, it's slow, thudding. I can't panic for three miles. I can't let anything take my breath away. Left arm, right arm. Breathe under the crook of my elbow. And then I do it again. Over, over, over again.

I swim.

Sailors call the ocean She. *She's rough today. She'll spit you out in a boat like that.* A long time ago, someone named this sea the Liberan, after the goddess of mothers and daughters. Maybe the sea-namers meant it as a comfort. Maybe they meant to imply that these waters would cradle and protect, as mothers are meant to.

Shivers of silver fish dart in my periphery. Sickle-shaped fins cut the water so near me, I'm glad I can't see better. When my skin starts to burn, I know I've been brushed by another jellyfish. All the while, the waves wash against me, so I breathe on their crests, kick in their troughs, and hope I'm going the right way. There's nothing to do but keep swimming. If I miss Providence, I'll die. If I give up before I reach it, I'll die. If I don't swim, I'll die.

The ocean reminds me, not of most mothers, but of my own. I swim.

I swim until the world beneath me starts to pale with dust and leaves. Until I can smell something other than ocean on the breeze—smoke. Trees. Until my hands are touching kelp, my knees are scraping sand, my cheek is pressed against chipped shells and pebbles of solid earth. Between two fingers, I take a piece of kelp that's washed up on shore, just like me. It's still slimy. I hold one of its air bladders, and *pop!* I've seen otters cling to buoyant kelp rafts before, tangling themselves within the forest to keep from floating away into an edgeless sea. Something to keep them safe. Something to keep them still.

See, Clementine? See, Bauer? I don't need either of you. Just watch.

I start to laugh, and then I start to cry.

CHAPTER TWO

THEN

SIX YEARS OLD

VALONIA, ASTORIAN ISLANDS

Eight years before my father died, he taught me to swim.

The water was a heavy sort of cold, the kind that makes your skin go so numb, you feel like just bones, a skeleton among the fish. Cliffs, stained white from all the seabirds and dotted with nests, towered above us. We lived in a house on top of those cliffs, but it was easy to forget about that down here, where the fog deadened all city sounds and made the whoosh of waves echo.

There was something magic about the ocean—or maybe something magic about me when I was *in* the ocean—that I hadn't yet tried to put words to. An expansiveness. A mystery. Later, I'd call it *possibility,* and I'd realize I'd always been greedy for it.

"Can you hold your breath, Thea-fish?" my father asked.

For a year, I'd been asking my parents to teach me to swim. In the bathtub, I'd practiced holding my breath, counting the seconds as my eyes began to burn. When Clementine swam the length of the shore, stretching her arms long and knifing through the water, I sat among the tide pools, knees hugged to my chest, and watched. Her arms looked like pale shark fins. She wore only knickers and a camisole, and once, when she came out of the water, blond hair streaming and cheeks bright, I heard the neighbor man suck in a breath. He was a commodore in the navy, a single father with a quiet, awkward son about my age, and the two of them had clambered down to shore to skip stones. When I saw the commodore shielding his son, as though Clementine had done something wrong, I felt incandescent indignity. Clementine strode out of the water like a goddess born from seafoam. The commodore ushered his son back up the rickety stairs, but Clementine just gave me a conspiratorial smile and, affecting a posh accent, said, "What rebels those Fowler women are."

To be part of a matched set with Clementine? There was no higher honor.

She swam every day. Even when it rained. Even when lightning ignited the sky and my father told me I wasn't allowed to sit outside. On those days, I watched from the windows. My father never tried to tell Clementine she couldn't swim; it didn't occur to me that other husbands might.

Finally, finally, I convinced them I was ready to don my bathers and learn. My father held me afloat in waist-deep water. Clementine was farther out, slicing silently through the waves. I watched her over my father's shoulder.

I took a deep breath. Stuck my face in the ache-cold water and blew bubbles through my nose. I opened my eyes and got my first glimpse of the underside of the world: moon-scaled fish and craggy coral and the churn of shells and sand.

When I came up, my father beamed.

I'd always been greedy for possibility, but my want was more exact than that. I wanted to be someone for whom anything was possible. I wanted to be someone who didn't accept the word *no* and invented herself as ever she pleased.

"There you go," my father said. "Just like your mother."

CHAPTER THREE

THEN

TEN YEARS OLD

VALONIA, ASTORIAN ISLANDS

In my tenth autumn, Keswick-Fleming School for Boys accepted their first female pupil.

Everyone knew the university never turned down a Keswick-Fleming man.

I had hoped, when Clementine told me it was time for my studies to get serious, that she would teach me. She told me—sympathetically, I think—that she needed time for her own research, never mind that no one ever published it.

Keswick-Fleming: red brick; bright grass. A statue of Saleus, the god of the seas from Classical myth, towered above the entrance. Me in a starchy white dress, surrounded by a sea of rolled-up black sweater sleeves and loose ties and mussed hair. The classrooms stank of chalk and formaldehyde and the teachers made me stand outside when they lectured on human anatomy.

But.

I had stacks of notebooks and neat little dissection knives and studying to call my own. I had ink stains on my hands and the gift of Clementine's sly smile when I came home in the afternoons. I even had a friend, Wes Price, whom I finally forgave for his commodore father's rudeness on our shared bit of shoreline. On my first day, Wes let me use his textbook when the mathematics instructor tried to make me do problems from a book for seven-year-olds.

In the time I studied at Keswick-Fleming, there were days that were truly, spectacularly happy. Like my twelfth birthday, when my father made me a cake with the honey he collected from our backyard hive, and Clementine surprised me with a painting she'd done of a sea otter, and Wes climbed over the fence to eat dinner with us. Clementine quizzed Wes and me about what we were learning, and my father smeared frosting on her nose, and Wes's dog, missing him, leaped through an open window and knocked Wes out of his chair. It was chaos, and *merry,* and in those moments, I began to feel like anything was possible. Like my future was an adventure I would find.

But there had been a timer filling with sand. I didn't know it, but it was there all along. Counting down the good days. Now, looking back, I see everything under the shadow of that timer. *Eight years before. Four years before. One year before.*

Zero.

CHAPTER FOUR

THEN

FOURTEEN YEARS OLD

VALONIA, ASTORIAN ISLANDS

My parents were fighting.

Again.

We were crammed together in a carriage, heading to Grandpa and Grandma Morgan's house for dinner. Just before we'd left, the windows had rattled in their panes—one more in a long line of tremors that, according to Clementine, portended volcanic doom.

"I don't want to see my father," Clementine said, folding her arms over her chest. She was wearing a black silk dress, and I wore indigo, and our combined skirts took up enough room to make the carriage feel small. "If he *still* won't publish my paper, despite the fact that this is a public safety crisis—"

"If public safety were your concern," my father said, "you'd let me publish it under my name."

"I did more than half the research," Clementine snapped.

"I'm not saying it's fair! I'm just saying that—"

"You can't force me to get along with him, you know,"

Clementine said. "He's a mean, backward old man, and he's never thought I was worth anything more than spitting out children."

I curled back in my seat. Usually, this would be the point where one or both of my parents would remember I was there. Soften. Change the conversation.

But this was a fight that had been brewing my whole life.

"I'm not siding with your father! Clem, come on."

"Mount Telamon is going to erupt," Clementine said stubbornly. "You know it. I know it. *Thea* knows it. And nobody will believe me because—what? *Because I'm a woman?*"

I wished I could sink into the upholstery. As I'd gotten older, I'd realized two things.

One: That I liked science, with or without my parents' interference. They may have nudged—or shoved—me toward it, but science and I got along. The organization of chaos into logic. The threads connecting everything. The way I could stand in the ocean and know why it was blue and why fish had gills and where these currents were traveling. Science was a family mantle I could carry; a tradition that bound me to Clementine and my father and even Grandpa Morgan.

Two: That I would never be able to study it.

Oh, maybe I could study like Clementine. But not like my father. Not like Grandpa Morgan.

Clementine probably hoped times would've changed more between her school years and mine. That by the time I was old enough for the university, they would've started accepting girls.

They hadn't. Even the teachers at Keswick-Fleming seemed increasingly suspicious of me as I grew.

I wanted a life of possibility, but the more I imagined life beyond Keswick-Fleming, the less I saw.

"Please," my father said, sounding tired. "Let's just talk to Rupert one more time. Beg him to take this seriously. Maybe if I'm with you—"

Clementine slammed her palm against the wall of the carriage. "Stop the horses," she called, and the driver did. I banged my elbow against the wall. Steadied myself.

"You want to talk to him?" she said. "Go by yourself."

My father rubbed his eyes, exhaling slowly. "Fine. Fine." He opened the carriage door, then glanced back, met my eye. Pressed a quick kiss to my forehead. "Back soon, Thea-fish."

Clementine was silent as he got out of the carriage. My father told the driver to take us back home; that he'd walk the rest of the way to the Morgans'.

The carriage jostled back into motion.

"You know," Clementine said, "in the Classical era, some women served as oracles. They sat in caves and breathed hallucinogenic fumes and predicted the future to travelers."

"And . . . ?" I said.

"Sounds nice."

"To breathe hallucinogenic fumes?"

She tipped her head back and stared skyward like she was picturing the stars beyond the carriage. "To be believed."

. . .

I was in the bath when the next tremor struck.

Not a tremor this time but a quake. The water sloshed out of the tub, soaking the floor, and I grabbed the lip of the porcelain to steady myself. The indigo dress sat rumpled on the tile, damming a wave of water.

The whole house rattled. I kept bits of sea glass on the edge of my sink, and one by one, all of them *clink clink clinked* to the floor. By the time it ended, my heart was in my throat.

A funny thing about earthquakes—when you're in one, it's hard to imagine the epicenter was anywhere else.

"Thea Fowler?"

The news found me at school the next day. Science class.

I turned from my textbook to the door, where one of the secretaries—one of the only women who worked at Keswick-Fleming—held a piece of paper between her hands. Her eyes were wide and panicked. Wet, almost.

"What?" I said. "What's wrong?"

She handed me the paper.

"Oh," I said. "I don't . . . ?"

Flash:

I was on the ground, staring at the ceiling. Blood on the back of my head. Sticky, like tack.

Flash:

"Thea!" Wes on the floor beside me. I stared up at the boys, a ring above me, a murder of crows in their black sweaters.

Flash:

The science teacher pressed a tonic into my hands. It was thick as syrup, tingling as it oozed down my throat. When I looked at the cup, my tongue all coated in tonic, I saw a lacy wing caught in the viscous ruby surface. Dragonfly, I thought. Dragonfly wing.

Wes took me home from school, I think, though I don't really remember it. I'm sure he asked if I wanted him to stay, and I'm sure I pushed him away, because I remember walking the echoey halls of my house alone. As the sun sank, I wondered if it was actually me who was dead, a ghost haunting the shell of this place, no longer able to see the living beings who owned it.

I found Clementine in her painting studio, the windows flung open. She was covered in paint. Fingernails, face, hair, dress. All bloody with cadmium and naphthol. She usually painted carefully, but that day's canvas was as big as the whole wall, messy and gooey. I stared at it for a long time before I was able to make sense of the overlapping pinks and reds. It was a set of raw lungs, deflated, and a heart, oozing, and a stomach, distended with blood.

Clementine never told me *When your father died, I felt like someone reached inside of me and ripped everything out.*

She put her painted hand on my shoulder and said, "You and me, kid."

. . .

Clementine's parents brought us a bouquet of mourning flowers so big, I couldn't see Grandpa Morgan's head around it. I tried to let them through the front door, but Clementine intercepted us. She held the door with one hand and the frame with the other, barring entry.

"You can't blame us for what happened," Grandpa Morgan said.

"He was at *your* house!" Clementine snapped.

"The whole wall fell," Grandpa Morgan said. "It could've been any of us. Or *all* of us."

"If only."

Grandma Morgan recoiled. Grandpa just sighed. "Be reasonable, Clem."

"Don't call me that. And I've always been reasonable. These earthquakes are just more proof that Mount Telamon is going to—"

"Phin's hardly cold and you're already back to ranting about that?" Grandpa Morgan said.

Clementine stiffened. I reached for her arm, seeking solidarity, and I found it.

"Go," Clementine said coldly. "Now."

"Come stay with us," Grandma Morgan said. "You shouldn't grieve alone."

"If you're worrying about my safety," Clementine said, "stop. I have a gun."

Grandma Morgan's face crinkled with disapproval. She was tall, like Clementine, and I had to look up at her. "Then do it for propriety's sake."

"Goodbye," Clementine said, closing the door.

"At least let us take Thea!"

Grandpa Morgan's words were lost behind the door, shut.

Clementine looked down at me. "You're right, Thea," she said, even though I hadn't said a thing. "We're never going to care about propriety again."

One week. One week between my father's death and the end of everything.

There were no signs. Clementine's upper lip was stiff. When we saw each other, it wasn't *You and me, kid*. It was like we were two guests at a hotel, dancing past each other in the hallway, each living our separate, lonely lives. I was grieving; she was plotting.

"Can't you just talk to her?" Wes asked.

We were lying on the floor of the Prices' skiff, our arms pressed together. Everything hurt and nothing was the same, but there was Wes. There was Wes, who'd loved my father too, and who'd lost his own mother as an infant. Wes, who understood when I said I felt like there was a ship sitting on my chest, like I'd never breathe again. Wes, who was a pocket of warmth that I dared believe might be enough to push away the grief, if only I could get close enough.

"She doesn't want to talk to me," I said. "Besides, if I told her I felt . . ." *Sad* was too small a word. "I don't know. I don't want to sound hysterical. Or irrational."

"Grieving doesn't make you hysterical *or* irrational," Wes said.

The skiff rocked gently. The night sky above, the rhythmic sea below, and us, trapped between two infinities.

"Can we talk about something else?" I said.

"Which constellation is that?" He pointed east in the wilderness of stars.

"The whale," I said, grateful for a distraction. "Baelenes."

"And that one?" he asked.

"That's Thea. You know that one. See her spear?"

"And—"

His finger was fixed on some geometry of light, but where, I didn't see. My face had drifted from the sky, and his too. Our noses were close enough to brush. I could count each dark eyelash and freckle on his face.

I just wanted this feeling to *go away*.

I just wanted to feel like I had a future.

Before I could move, I heard Clementine yell from the porch. I sat up with a start. "I should go."

"Thea, are you—"

I ran.

That was as close to goodbye as we ever got.

The next morning, Clementine woke me at dawn. "The carriage is waiting."

"Waiting? For what? Where are we going?"

"Away," she said. "Before the eruption."

"I haven't packed anything."

"I packed everything you need," she said. "Come on."

I rubbed my eyes with the heels of my hands. For a minute, in my half-sleep, I'd forgotten about my father. When I remembered, grief and guilt hit me in the same breath. I dropped my hands. Gazed around my room. There were my school notebooks; my collection of Classical myths; my soft crimson robe. I didn't take any of them, maybe because I'd fallen prey to the same thing that captured Grandpa Morgan and everyone else who tried to deny Clementine. Because I didn't believe her. Not enough, anyway.

We would only be gone a few weeks, surely, and Clementine was in a hurry, so I pulled a simple yellow dress over my head, laced my boots, and followed her to the carriage. Empty-handed.

"Where are we going?" I asked as we bumped down the path. "To the country? East Valonia?"

"Not far enough," Clementine said.

"One of the other islands, then?"

She didn't respond. She was staring out the window, caught in a web of her own thoughts.

My palms started to itch. Something felt *not right* about this, the same way not mentioning my father felt not right. The same way everything had felt not right since he died. We weren't meant to be just two, Clementine and me. Our family had always been a triangle, balancing each other, and now we were vertexless.

The carriage rolled to a stop at the harbor.

Outside, the air was cold with morning. It smelled like the fishing nets heaped on the docks.

"That's ours," Clementine said, pointing. I followed her finger.

A large ship. A merchant ship. Grandpa Morgan's parents had been merchants, and I knew he still kept a few of their old ships running. Not that any of the Astorian Islands grew much worth trading anymore. But I recognized this as one of his.

On the deck, a handful of sailors were already moving around. Doing what, I had no idea. I'd never sailed.

"What are you talking about? What's going on?"

Clementine picked up her trunk. Her jaw was set. A gust of wind whipped by, and her hair snapped like a sail. "They'll die not believing me," she said. "I've decided to let them."

CHAPTER FIVE

THEN

FOURTEEN YEARS OLD

LIBERAN SEA

Mount Telamon erupted four days later.

The whole sky turned black. Soot coated the ship in shadow snow. Some of the crew slid across it, spinning like ice-skaters.

From fleeing ships, we learned that lava had swallowed most of Valonia. The rest of the Astorian Islands, sparsely populated but crucial in keeping us fed, were protected by sea from the molten rock but not from the ash. They vanished under thick, black clouds of it. Nothing would grow again; not for a long time. And just like that, the Astorian Islands were empty. What people weren't killed fled to the continent—to a stretch of shore once filled with Astorians, back before the gods decided to curse us and before everything we touched turned to ruin.

I sat in the choking soot-fall and cried. Hot, angry tears for Wes and my grandparents and my father's body, already dead but still deserving better. For my home and the sea birds, my father's bees and my old book of myths. For a dream of studying science and understanding the world, understanding how I was connected to it. All my connections were snipped, slashed, burned.

All except the thread that tethered me to Clementine.

"Oh, Thea," she said when she found me. She stared at the cloud of smoke on the horizon with a vindictive smile, like the volcano was an old enemy she was pleased to defeat. "None of that. Our lives are just beginning."

Chapter Six

Then

Fifteen years old

LIBERAN SEA

A new beginning, Clementine said, and if it were one of the myths, it would've gone like this:

Then and now and then, a pirate queen ruled the Liberan Sea. Once, she had been a scholar's daughter and a scholar's widow, but no one remembered anymore.

If you asked a sailor in a tavern about Captain Clementine Fowler's daughter, they would probably think you meant her ship, *Asterope's Revenge,* because Clementine's true daughter was a rotten pirate, and every day, that daughter felt more and more shame.

Then and now and then, a pirate daughter realized she would never be as great as her mother.

I never saw Valonia again. There was nothing left worth taking at the ash-choked Astorian Islands, and no people, either. All that was left of that once great civilization was a trio of settlements: Providence, Silver Creek, and Fairshore. Three settlements of a few hundred people each. They would've been stronger together, but too many men wanted to play governor. That's what Clementine said, at least. From the crew, I heard that cities farther inside the continent didn't like to trade with Astorians. Maybe because Astorians were haughty and insular, so why should anyone bother helping them? Maybe because Astorians had nothing worth trading.

Maybe it was just because this stretch of coast was plagued by pirates.

Being on Clementine's crew meant ransacking trading ships and fishing boats alike. It meant scanning Astorian faces with equal parts hope and dread. It meant watching the mates get drunk at Tanager Rock, an outpost, and watching Clementine strike a tenuous peace with other pirate captains at Saleus Cove during the autumn armistice.

Being Clementine's daughter meant that just being on her crew wasn't enough.

By her second year of piracy, Clementine had realized she was as good at this as she was at everything, and suddenly, being merely a captain wasn't enough. So she told the crew to head to Providence, one of the languishing little settlements. They had an old Astorian naval ship, recently repaired, and Clementine wanted it. She would give it to Livia, her quartermaster.

Clementine wanted a fleet.

And who would captain the third ship? Cadmus. Benjy. Any of the mates, any of the sailors, *anyone* but me, whom the crew mostly ignored and who still got seasick and who cared more about tides and dolphins than guns and battle.

"I don't . . ." I tried to tell her. "I can't . . ."

"If you want to be a captain," Clementine told me, "you need to prove yourself. Show the crew you're not afraid to take care of yourself."

"What's that supposed to mean?"

We were on *Asterope's* deck, wind whipping my hair everywhere. The inside of my throat felt dry from the sea.

"You can take care of yourself, can't you?" she asked.

"Like how?"

"Like if someone points a gun at you, you shoot faster."

I swallowed. "Clementine, I don't—"

"Do you know what happens to women who can't stand up for themselves? Who aren't every bit as strong as men? They die, Thea. They die in childbirth. On surgery tables. At the hands of men. They die of diseases no one has bothered to study because they're *women's conditions*. Women die, and die, and die. And I know you think I'm cruel now, making you do this. But you are not a statistic. You're my daughter. And you know what? As long as you survive, I don't care if you think I'm the cruelest bitch who ever walked the earth." A pause. "And you'll make a damn good captain."

I never did learn how to say no to Clementine.

We arrived in Providence to steal Livia's ship a week later. I'd never been so close to one of the settlements. Never been close enough to imagine myself walking among those people, living in these buildings.

Providence: It was a skeleton with the wrong skin.

Relics remained from ancient Astorians: white columns with no roofs left to support; chipped marble statues of the gods; a tiled market square. Beyond the ruins, a dark forest rose from the hillside.

The ship in the harbor was beautiful—long and lean, with perfect sails and a gleam on the hull that made clear how much it mattered to someone.

The year I'd sailed on *Asterope* should've inured me to the reality of piracy. We fired guns and brandished knives. We tried to scare people so they'd give up their ships more quickly. We fought viciously, and they fought desperately. Rarely did anyone have backup coming. Rarely did anyone have enough manpower or firepower to fight back well.

Providence, though, was even worse than usual.

As we approached the harbor, it became clear that this ship might've once belonged to the Astorian navy, but there was no navy left. How few people had survived the eruption? I still didn't know. By the time we reached the harbor, a group of settlers, men and women alike, stood on the deck, weapons raised. Axes, swords, kitchen knives. Battered bits of wood. I counted only two guns. The settlers stared back at us, our guns, our salivating crew, with looks of resigned determination.

But still, they fought.

I wish they wouldn't have.

I tried to leave. I made it halfway back across the deck, hoping I could escape below. A hand caught my shoulder. Clementine.

"What are you doing?" she said.

"I don't want to see anyone I know."

She crouched slightly so we were the same height. Behind us, gunshots rang. "You left them behind," she said. "They have no power over you."

Clementine marched me back to the railing. I faced the settlers, but I couldn't fire. Their faces flashed in front of me. None familiar. Was I relieved? Maybe. But it meant everyone I knew probably died in the eruption.

Just as well.

Five minutes of fighting, and only one settler remained on their fine, fine ship. Everyone else was dead on the deck, or tumbling into the water, or running back to the harbor. But that man, that one man, he was still holding his too-small knife aloft.

"Do the honors," Clementine said.

It took me a minute to realize what she meant. *Do the honors.* Kill him.

"What?" I said. No, no, *no no no*—

"Remember what I said about opportunity?" Clementine replied.

"I don't—"

Bang.

The man dropped.

Smoke curled from Livia's gun. She slipped it back in her holster, and the crew began to cheer.

I moved across the ship like a sleepwalker.

There was nothing, nothing on this wide ocean, that I wanted more than to slip out of my skin and be someone other than myself.

As Clementine and Livia readied their ships, their fleet, to sail, I watched Providence. A few of the settlers watched me back. I saw a boy standing halfway behind a crumbling column. He shielded his face to the sun.

I'm sorry. I'm sorry.

Then his hand dropped.

It wasn't.

Oh, it was.

I pressed my stomach to the railing and watched him, watched his disbelief crumble into betrayal, his betrayal calcify into rage.

If I had hoped I could be someone other than Clementine's daughter, pirate-in-training, that hope died when Wes looked at me. And shook his head.

We sailed away and left the settlement to die.

I snuck into Clementine's cabin that night, even though I wasn't supposed to. The captain's quarters were off-limits, but there was nowhere else private to cry on *Asterope's Revenge,* and my tears were catastrophic and unstoppable. I curled sideways on Clementine's bed. The tears fell frantically, and I rubbed them away with furious panic. I pulled at my hair and screamed under my breath.

I just wanted all of my feelings to *stop*.

Two weeks prior, I'd gotten my first period, and though according to one of Clementine's anatomy textbooks, that made me a late bloomer, I still didn't feel like I'd had enough time to prepare. Did anyone ever? I hadn't told Clementine. It felt like such a delicate, embarrassing, feminine matter. I wasn't sure how, or why, but it felt like I'd done something wrong. Like my body had conceded to the fact that I might someday be a mother—a job my own mother seemed to resent, even if she didn't resent me, exactly. So I'd asked Livia for help instead. Livia had given me some spare underwear and towels. Nothing ever embarrassed Livia; that was probably why Clementine liked her so much.

I felt like I was growing up, and not. Like I would be forever frozen at the age I was when my father died and we left Valonia. Like I both was and could never again be the person who had not said goodbye to Wes Price.

The door creaked.

I looked up, and there was Clementine. When she saw me in her bed, she started to frown. Then she noticed the tears and she just shook her head, confused, and shut the door behind her.

"What's the matter with you?" she asked. Not cruelly. She didn't mean it as an insult. It was a genuine question. What *was* the matter with me? I'd decided long ago that I needed to be Clementine in miniature, so why couldn't I just be that person? I was supposed to be strong, like the goddess Thea from all the myths. Not like Libera, the goddess of childbirth and weepy emotion.

"This is stupid," I said. "I don't want to be on this ship. I want to go home."

"Home is gone," Clementine said.

I wanted it anyway. I wanted to go back to Wes, even though he hated me. I never wanted to stare at the ocean again for as long as I lived.

"Please," I said quietly. "I don't belong here."

"Of course you do," she said, sitting on the bed next to me. She didn't touch me, but she touched the quilt next to me. I just wanted her to reach out. Hug me. Do something.

"I don't," I say. "I'm not a pirate, Clementine. I'm not good at this. I should be in the settlement with—"

"You saw him," she said.

I flinched.

She shut her eyes for a moment, inhaled, and said, "The *Valonians*. You want to go back to the *Valonians*. Because you miss a boy."

My cheeks went hot. "No, it wasn't—not with Wes, it wasn't like that."

"Don't you see, Thea? I gave you freedom. I spent my whole life trying to be heard. No one ever listened because I was a *wife* and a *mother* and a *woman*. You don't have to worry about that. What boy can compare to freedom?"

I shook my head. How could I explain that it wasn't about Wes?

Freedom, she said, like I didn't understand. I'd always wanted freedom. *Possibility.*

Possibility died on *Asterope's Revenge.*

"The only thing I'm free to choose," I said, "is which of your pirate ships I sail on."

She eyed me for a minute. Considering. "How many people do you think died in the eruption?"

I let out a breath. Stared at the ceiling. "Can you talk in a straight line? Please? For once?"

"Thousands," she said, ignoring me. "When so many lives are destroyed, what do you think they care about? The men in charge. Repopulation. Preserving lineages, property. You want to go back to the settlements? Enjoy being a reproductive commodity."

I was suddenly a thousand times more aware of my body's betrayal: that first period.

"Then please," I said. "Let's go someplace else. We can go farther into the continent. Leave the sea behind. We never need to see another Astorian again."

"And do *what,* exactly? Do you speak any other languages? Do you know any trades? Do you have any idea what the rest of the world thinks of us, the insular Astorians in our lonely, cursed corner of the sea? We've never been kind to the rest of the world, and they've never been kind to us, and I'm not about to ask them to start. We're not living on land, Thea. We have a good life here, and I made it for both of us." Her eyes roved across me. When I didn't respond, she said, "You're welcome."

Still, I said nothing.

"Stop crying," she said, almost desperately. For all of her cleverness, I was the puzzle she couldn't solve. "You know what a man is when he cries?" she said. "He's *sensitive*. He's an *artist*. You know what a woman is, when she shows her feelings? Another teary woman. She's *weak*. A man is strong for showing his feelings. A woman is strong for killing hers."

"I want to," I said. "Please, help." The weight of sadness was big and intrusive inside me, like I'd swallowed rocks. Couldn't she see how much I wanted to stop crying? Stop *feeling*? It wasn't that I didn't want to be a pirate. It was that I didn't want to be me, who was so bad at it.

I just wanted to be like Clementine. *Please*.

"The world wants to hurt you," she said. "The world doesn't care about your voice. Doesn't that make you angry?"

"Of course it does," I said.

"Get angry, Thea!" she said, voice rising. "Get angry!"

"I am angry!" I said, and I was—my face was covered in angry tears, and I was shouting from the exhaustion of not being heard. I lived in a box of one-way mirrors where everyone could see me and everyone could shout at me and nothing I did ever seemed to make an impression on anyone else.

"Not like that!" she shouted back. "Not . . . not hysterical."

"Then tell me the right way to be!"

She narrowed her eyes at me, the way she would look at a sail in need of replacement. Looking for the cracks in my armor, the flaws in my design. She found, apparently, too many.

"I have a ship to captain," she said, and she left me without another word.

To the empty, open door, I whispered, "Tell me the right way to be. Please."

She didn't respond; she already had. She'd named me Thea.

CHAPTER SEVEN

NOW

SEVENTEEN YEARS OLD

PROVIDENCE

Providence sprawls before me.

All the soot- and sea-stained marble.

The statues.

I remember the place I saw Wes, standing in the shadow of a column reaching nowhere. Maybe I should've jumped off *Asterope's Revenge* then. Begged for forgiveness. Well, it's too late now.

I haul myself out of the water and scrub the tears from my face. My eyes are probably too red from the salt for a few minutes of self-indulgent crying to make a difference, but I want the tears gone all the same.

The ocean gazes back at me. I can't see the *Pelican* on the horizon.

I'm starting to wonder if I shouldn't just turn around and go for another five- to ten-mile swim. Now that I've made it, I realize that the question of *will my body hold up* staved off the question of *will my mind hold up*. But now that I'm here, trying to be still, the force of that question hits me.

What am I *doing* here?

I'm in a tiny settlement with no allies, no home, no food. I'm soaking wet, freezing cold, and so thirsty, I can't swallow without a burn in my throat. I ran away from Clementine, and then I ran away from Bauer, and now I'm here, and unless I want to die, I need to figure out what to do next.

What would Clementine do?

Survive. The answer comes easily. She'd survive, so that's what I'll do too.

The number of ways in which I am near death is oddly comforting. It gives me purpose. First: water. Second: fire, to dry off and warm up. Third: shelter, so I can sleep somewhere safe. The basic, animal requests my body is making are easy to obey.

And after I stop myself from dying? What then? I can't go back to Clementine. We didn't part on the best terms. We didn't part on any terms, really—she spouted cruelty and I was too weak to take it, so I ran while she slept, like a coward. If I ask for her forgiveness, she won't give it.

But I don't know who I am without her.

I push her from my head. First, survive. Later, worry about Clementine.

The clarity of a next step helps me breathe. I take inventory of myself and my surroundings. Myself: Hair so tangled I may never unsnarl it, but for now, the best I can do is a messy bun to get the cold lump of it off my neck. Feet shoeless, but at least I have my socks. My hands are white and purple with cold. The skin under my armpits oozes blood where my sleeves rubbed, but I don't have anything else to wear, so I'll have to live with it. My teeth chatter; I should get moving if I want to warm up.

My surroundings: A few storefronts glow in front of the harbor, and I think I can smell cooking food on the wind. It must be early afternoon, but there's so much fog that I can't tell where the sun is in the sky. I can see the whole of Providence from my vantage point on the beach, just a thumbnail of civilization carved from the expanse of virgin forest. There's a crumbling lighthouse on one cliff; a few bereft houses on another. Probably fifty buildings total. It's impossible to tell which of the old shells are occupied and which are still abandoned. They all look like relics.

Somewhere, in those fifty buildings, people I might know are going about their days. Is my grandmother working on delicate embroidery? Is the baker taking a batch of hot nautilus rolls from the oven? Is Wes braiding kelp by the tide pools?

Or maybe they're all dead.

I'm worried that I'll see someone I know, but I'm just as worried that I won't. I'm worried that I don't belong here, but I'm more worried that I don't belong anywhere. I'm worried that Clementine will show up, see me bedraggled and starving, and say, *Did you really think you could survive without me?*

I *will* survive without her. I've made it this far, haven't I?

If she comes here to find me, she'll find someone who doesn't need her help.

First, survive.

I start to walk. Each step, like each stroke in the ocean, kills the panic. Over, over, over again, step, step, step, I walk to survival.

The main street of Providence is situated between a wide river and the harbor. In the river, beige foam and clumps of algae swirl. I walk its length until I find a tributary: a brook coming from the east. When I don't see anything that looks like human waste, I deem it good enough. I may regret this in a few hours, but I'm too thirsty to haul myself any farther upstream. I drop to my knees and plunge my head in the water.

It's colder than the ocean. Sharp, quick cold. I drink, and drink, and drink. It tastes metallic, and my skin sings in pain. Good pain. Pain that says *You're doing this to stay alive.*

The water doesn't fill the empty cavern of my stomach. Next, food.

I glance around the brook. Plants with brambled branches and diamond-shaped leaves overhang the water. Keswick-Fleming taught botany, but I never loved plants the way I loved studying animals. Clementine liked to paint the plants around our house in Valonia, but even what little I remember from those lessons won't help me now. The climate is different here, on the edge of the continent. These plants could be luxurious, energy-dense roots as easily as they could be poisonous berries.

The smell of cooking food wafts from Providence again. I

look back at the glow of the harbor. I have no money. I don't even know what currency Providence uses—the old Astorian coins and bills or something new. And I don't want to plead. I don't want anyone in town to see how vulnerable I am right now.

Stealing, then.

I walk back to the harbor. In sunshine, it might be pleasant. But the fog sinks and sinks, weighing down the sky. It feels too quiet, too empty, for an afternoon, but maybe this is what it's always like in a settlement so small. A child skitters across the square, throwing me a nervous glance. I don't know whether to feel good or bad about that: being someone who inspires fear.

The shops are finely built but crudely repaired. It's going to take a long time to make a city that looks like Valonia again. Providence is a once great place, great no longer; a ghost of grandeur reanimated by a people who haven't yet figured out how to give up.

On my left, there's a stocky building with white walls and a sienna tiled roof. Where the walls have collapsed, they've been patched with wooden beams. The windows are rough and semi-opaque, more like sea glass than window glass, and they don't sit quite right in the frame. I squint through.

Vials of syrup and crushed leaves gleam in the hazy light. One is dark red, the color of rubies, and when I see it, my throat feels full of tar. I remember the science teacher pressing a tonic into my hands. I remember the taste of fermented berries and crushed dragonflies.

I press a hand to my lips. Backpedal.

The wind rakes through my hair. *Shh, shh,* off the ocean. With every moment that passes, the sky sags lower, *shh, shh.*

I follow my nose down the street until I find the source of the food smell. It's a tavern, not much larger than the apothecary. The chimney belches smoke.

A second ago, I was hungry, but I'm not sure I am anymore. Taverns remind me of Bauer. That smell, the greasy food and beer smell, makes me think of his hands, the big fingers around the delicate, sudsy glasses.

In my head, I hear Clementine's voice: *Stop being irrational. You'll keel over if you don't eat. You're really going to let the memory of some boy stop you from surviving?*

No, Clementine. I'm not.

I push open the door.

It's too smoky inside to breathe. My already scratched throat protests. I was hoping there would be—I don't know, a crowd, or something; but it's empty. No one to steal a plate from. No one whom I might pickpocket, if I knew how to do that.

I force myself to walk to the bar, where a vaguely familiar woman stands behind the counter. She blinks at me, like she's trying to remember if we've met. We might be the same age. Maybe we went to school together in Valonia before I left for Keswick-Fleming. She's round-faced, brown-skinned, a little wary.

"Can I get you something?"

"Food," I say.

"You're not from here," she says.

I take half a step back, bracing myself. Of course they don't have travelers here. Providence is surrounded on one side by mountains and on the other by pirate-infested seas. Only whalers and traders would ever wash through, but there are no such ships in the harbor, and besides, how many teenage girls sail with whalers? How many teenage girls have the stomach?

Not me, for one.

"Passing through," I say. And then, because she looks skeptical still, I add, "I can pay."

I don't know why I say it. I can't pay. Maybe I'm hoping she'll let me wash a few dishes to earn a meal. Maybe I'm hoping I can run when she's not looking. I haven't decided yet.

"Passing through?" she says, her voice light but not light enough to fool me. "From where?"

"Fairshore?" I hate how nervous I sound. "Fairshore."

"Your accent. You're Valonian. Me too."

I open my mouth.

Her eyebrows wrinkle. "Wait—you lived on the cliffs. I know you."

Then I recognize her. Diana. Di. I *do* remember her. We were in the same class until I was ten, and our fathers knew each other. Like mine, hers was a scholar at the university. Of humanities, I think, or maybe language.

If I remember that much about her, she probably remembers enough to know that I'm Clementine Fowler's daughter.

I take another step backward. *Don't say it. Don't say it.*

"Thea?" she says. "Thea Fowler?"

I run.

She calls over her shoulder—presumably for backup, in case I try anything—but before anyone else arrives, I hurtle outside.

My head is starting to swim from the hunger. The hunger, the smell. I go around the back of the tavern and find a trash heap. Flies, fishbones, chipped glass. I take a moldy heel of bread from the top. I try to tear off the bluest bit, but the bread is too stale to tear. So instead, I scrape it against the tavern wall until I think I've gotten the worst of it, and then I eat. I have to let it sit in my mouth for a count of ten before it's soft enough to chew. It tastes like sawdust.

Warmth at my back.

I leap out of the way.

A man stands over me, so tall that I dissolve in his shadow. Di's brother, maybe? I don't know if he's confused, if he's angry, if he's as startled as I am, because my eyes glide over his face and settle on his hands: big, covered in soap bubbles, holding a pair of half-washed glasses.

Stop being irrational, Clementine says, but more loudly, Bauer whispers, *You're scared, but I can protect you.*

I drop what's left of the bread and take off.

"Hey!" the man calls.

I don't stop.

I weave around the buildings, my stomach cramping. Black fringes my vision. I crouch, trying to steady myself on the edge of the street, where the stone turns to river. *Keep running. Come on, Thea.* My reflection, river-distorted, stares back at me.

The fat smell of the tavern hangs thick on the breeze. I hate that smell. It's sticking to me, infesting me. I want to jump back into the ocean. Burn these clothes. Burn my skin.

I vomit in the river.

My pilfered bread comes straight back up, hitting the dark water with such a disgusting splatter that I vomit again.

I stay like that too long. Hunched on the edge of the street. When the nausea starts to ebb, I try to get to my feet. The world sways.

White, chalky buildings spin before my eyes. I see the settlement, *flash,* as if from above: The buildings are brittle bones; this river is an artery. The settlement is a body, once left for dead, now slipped back into like a corpse-host for parasites.

The river water glimmers black beneath me. My reflection swims.

I stare back. Wipe my mouth with the heel of my hand.

Don't be hysterical.

Hysterical.

All the things I would do if I weren't afraid of being called hysterical. I would light this town on fire and draw pretty pictures in the ashes. I would scream until seventeen years of pent-up emotion left me. I would dress like a dragonfly, ruby red and gauzy, and I would laugh like everything was absolutely hysterical.

Oh—

I know I'm going to fall before I do.

There's a moment of quickening when I come back to myself. When the bones become buildings again; when I think, *You are a disaster, Thea. A catastrophe walking.*

Then I hit.

Not water. Something harder.

My vision goes bright white. Stars burst. I gasp.

I'm in the river, water tugging me downstream like flotsam. The bank is too steep to climb back out here, so I let myself be pulled toward the ocean. *This* is cold. Cold in a way that presses on my ribs and lungs like a corset laced too tight.

When I start to feel my heart pulsing in my skull, I drag one hand from the water. Touch my forehead. Warm. The only warm thing left on my body. I look at my fingers, and they're bloody.

By the time the bank levels out, I'm back at the ocean. It's hard not to take this as a sign. An hour ago, I was exhausted, but less a bout of vomiting and a head injury. Now I'm back where I started and worse off.

I crawl from the water. Shells dig into my hands and knees. Blood doesn't just drip, but *drains* from my forehead, puddling the shore beneath me.

Head injuries bleed. It's probably not that bad. And besides, I'm covered in water. That's diluting the blood. Making it look worse than it is.

I try to stand, and blood runs into my eyes.

"Damn all of this," I whisper. "Damn everyone."

I tear off my left sleeve. It takes a few fumbling attempts—my hands shake—but eventually, I bite the fabric and manage to free it. The wad of cloth is cool against my head.

Again, I face Providence.

You're being ridiculous.

A few years ago, these people were my fellow Astorians. Classmates, maybe. Neighbors. Friends. They might've grown to hate Clementine—might've hated Clementine all along— but I'm not with her anymore. I'm not with anyone anymore.

What am I trying to achieve, stumbling around and falling in rivers? *You won't always have a boy to come rescue you.* I don't want rescuing. Don't need it.

"Be rational," I tell myself.

Okay. Rational. I still need food and dry clothes and warmth, but most of all, I need bandages for my head and a mirror to survey the damage. An ointment to prevent infection, if possible.

I walk back in the direction of the apothecary whose window I stared through before. The ground spins unpredictably. To move, I cling to the side of one building until I reach its edge, then I leap to the next one, steadying myself against the new wall. My head is playing tricks on me. I keep thinking I hear whispers, but when I look around, the settlement is empty. No one in sight. Just me and my trail of blood.

When I reach the apothecary, I lean against the door, and it flies open. I stumble inside.

It's empty.

Dusky, purple light glitters against the vials in the window. On the counter, a mortar full of dried mushrooms sits next to a water-stained book, open to a recipe for an infection salve. For a brief moment, I consider trying to finish the recipe—I could use it for my forehead—but I can't even pick up the mortar. My whole body trembles.

I haul myself behind the counter. Here, there are rows upon rows of bottles. Rolled lengths of cloth. Everything is labeled in a cramped, slanting hand I can't read, but I grab a bandage and press it to my forehead. My sleeve is already soaked through.

"Sorry, apothecary," I say, picking a few of the bottles at random. "I wouldn't have taken so much if you'd labeled your shelves better."

Voices.

Loud voices.

"I tried my best, okay? I don't exactly have a lot to work with."

"Yes, I'm sure that will be a great comfort to his widow."

"If you would just—"

The door flies open.

Three glass bottles fall from my hands and shatter on the floor.

Wes Price is covered in blood.

He moves the same way he always did, stepping through the door. Willow graceful, with long limbs and delicate features—a thin mouth, a long nose just so. His skin at its palest was still a shade darker than my skin at its tannest. As a kid, he looked like the painting of his mother that hung in his house, but now, disconcertingly, I see Wes's father in the span of his shoulders and the length of his legs. I remember being the taller of the two of us.

I compress, compress, compress my feelings.

His shirt is white, sleeves rolled up, revealing a watch on one wrist and a ratty leather cord on the other.

Covered in blood.

It's a blossom across his stomach, up his sleeves and on his hands and across his cheeks. His dark hair is matted in places, and I imagine that's from blood too.

"If I would just what?" the other voice says, and then I see his father, Commodore Price, grinding to a halt in the doorway.

Wes, I haven't seen in a year. Commodore Price, I saw just a week ago. But they stare at me with identical expressions of shock.

The commodore is in better shape than he was last week— freshly shaven, though his clothes, like Wes's, are blood-stained.

"Did your mother send you?" Commodore Price says.

I open my mouth. Can't answer.

Both of the Prices step forward, and I step back, hitting the shelves. The bottles rattle behind me. Why are the Prices covered in blood? *Their* blood? No, it can't be theirs. Wes wouldn't be upright if he'd lost as much blood as stains his shirt. He'd be like me, frantic and dizzy.

"Where's Clementine?" Wes says, and oh, his voice is so *cold*. I shouldn't have expected anything else.

"I don't know," I say.

"What are you doing here?" Commodore Price says in the same moment Wes asks, "What happened to your head?"

"I swam. I fell. I'm just . . . why are you covered in blood?"

Commodore Price sets a protective hand on Wes's shoulder. In a low voice, he says, "I'll send someone to look for Clementine's ship. You can take care of her?"

Wes nods.

Take care of. Odd how a phrase that means *bandage her up and give her tea* can just as easily mean *bury her out back.*

The door swings shut behind Commodore Price.

"What are you stealing?" Wes asks. No warmth there, none. "What's your plan?"

Not bleed to death out of my head? It's funny to imagine that I look like someone who might have a plan.

"I'm not with Clementine," I manage. "She's not here."

"Then how did you get to Providence?"

"I swam."

"You swam from Clementine's ship?"

"No," I say. "From a different ship. A whaler."

Wes narrows his eyes at me. The force of him so clearly *not believing me* hits like a fist to my chest. But why would he believe me? I vanished without a word. Without a trace. Never wrote a letter because Clementine wouldn't have let me send it and never tried to visit because Clementine would've laughed at the idea.

"You asked why I was covered in blood," he says. "A sailor came back after a run-in with pirates. He died. If you were wondering."

"I don't know anything about that," I say. "It wasn't me."

He glances over his shoulder. Looking for what? Backup?

I can't stay here. Not with Wes eyeing me like I'm a stranger, an enemy, a snake about to bite. I keep my hand tight around the roll of bandages as I hobble out from behind the counter.

"Are you going to pay for those?" he says flatly.

He doesn't get out of my way, but he doesn't try to stop me, either. There's a deadness in his eyes that mirrors what I feel deep in my stomach. What's lonelier than looking at someone who shouldn't be a stranger, but is?

I go around him and push through the door. Maybe letting me run is one final nod to the friendship we once had. When I glance back over my shoulder, he's facing away, still staring at the counter. I can't see his face, but I watch his hands slowly clench, then fall open again, weary. With one long blood-stained finger, he touches the cord around his wrist, like I'm not the only one who spends all my life remembering.

CHAPTER EIGHT

NOW

SEVENTEEN YEARS OLD

PROVIDENCE

The sun has fully set by the time I find my way to a stretch of muddy beach at the edge of Providence. There are fewer buildings out here, spread like fish lost from the school. It smells like cypress, pine, and wild rosemary. Like solid, wet earth. Like hearth smoke from homes, little universes that may as well be a million miles away.

Hunger comes and goes in waves. It's gone now. I've thrown my bloodied sleeve into the ocean and tied the new bandages around my head. My mouth is still dry and my skin burns from salt. Occasionally, my transgressive brain drifts back to questions of Wes, like what he was doing in the apothecary, or what he was thinking when he touched the cord on his wrist. I try to silence them.

I suppose I'll sleep here, on the shore. This way, I'll be able to see any ships heading from the horizon. Will Clementine come after me? I told the whalers she wouldn't. Is it wrong that I hope she will?

Stop that.

Of course it's wrong to hope.

When I ran away from Clementine, I looked at her, asleep in her bed, and thought: *I will show you what I'm capable of.* It was a dare. At that point, I still thought she'd stop me.

What have I shown her I'm capable of so far? Trusting a boy I never should've trusted. Losing my voice when I should've shouted. And a damn long swim.

Footsteps behind me. I look over my shoulder, expecting, impossibly, to see Clementine. *Hoping* to see Clementine. Because without her, I am lost, small, weak.

But it's not Clementine. It's Hanna Bauer.

No—not Hanna *Bauer.* She's married. She probably has her husband's last name. I don't know what it is. To me, she's just Bauer's older sister, and it's so incongruous to see her anywhere but Tanager Rock that I lurch backward.

"Thea?" she says.

She's pregnant. Her cream cotton dress bulges below her ribs. It's easier to look at that, the dress, because I'd forgotten how much her face looks like Bauer's—the wheat-gold curls; the pink lips; the geometric jaw. She's as pretty as he was. Is.

"What are you doing here?" I ask. My voice sounds scratchy. I wish I would've chosen something more eloquent to use it for. Maybe: *Leave me alone,* or: *I hate your whole fucking family.*

"I live here," she says. "What are you doing here?"

I look down at myself. Blood-spattered clothes. Fingers turning indigo from cold. "Sunbathing."

"Are you . . . you know, *okay?*"

"I'm breathing, aren't I?"

"But did someone hurt you?" she asks, which is a funny question. *Yes. Your brother.*

"No," I snap.

She sets a gentle hand on my shoulder, and I leap to my feet to get out from under her touch. "I can see it in your eyes."

I don't want hurt written in my eyes. I refuse it. I hate that someone else has the power to hurt me; the power to do anything to me. Clementine taught me that there are only two types of people: the powerful and the powerless. And I won't be powerless. I won't let Hanna touch my shoulder gently and tuck my hair behind my ear. I won't let her tell me she can see the hurt in my eyes. Smiling sadly like she's waiting for me to shatter.

This is your fault, I think. *You could've warned me.*

"Why don't you come back to my house?" Hanna says. "And we can figure out how to get you back to your mother."

At that, I feel something in me shift, seismic.

I don't want to go back to *my mother.*

My mother, who told me I had to be a scientist, who told me I had to go to Keswick-Fleming, who told me I had to be a pirate. My mother, who has never cared what I wanted a day in her life. If Clementine loved me, she wouldn't have tried to force me to kill people, and then maybe I never would've run away with Bauer, and then he wouldn't have betrayed me, and then none of us would be in this mess.

I've been blaming myself, all my life, really, but now I see the truth, sharp and clear:

Clementine is a pirate and a thief and a murderer.

And just once, I want to make her feel as small as she makes me.

My panic grows quiet under a tide of anger, and the anger feels *so much better.*

"No," I say again, not sharply this time, but cold, calm.

There are only two types of people: the powerful and the powerless. I am not lost; I am not small; I am not weak without Clementine.

I don't need her. I only need myself.

Get angry, Thea! I hear her shouting. *Get angry!*

"Where does Commodore Price live?" I ask.

"Pardon?" Hanna says, blinking.

I don't repeat myself. I just stand, inhale, fill my chest with heat. It's a righteous sort of anger, and it lights me up like fire. Fear brought me nothing. Anger is a tool I can wield.

"The big house on the southern cliffs," Hanna says. "The one with the statue of Saleus in the front. But don't you think—"

I make her go quiet with a glance. I could never do that before. Clementine could. One look from her narrowed, angry eyes, and anyone's mouth would snap shut. And now I know the secret. The fire.

One of the last things Clementine said to me was *Are you my daughter or not?*

Oh, Clementine. I am your daughter. I am so, completely your daughter.

And I will show you what my fire can do.

. . .

Providence smells like beached seals. The fishing ships are docked, sails furled. A pair of seagulls won't shut up.

The anger fills my empty stomach even better than food could. It's like I've discovered a new form of sustenance. I'm a plant, photosynthesizing fury. My vision pulses red at the edges. I see the house on the top of the cliffs at the southern side of Providence, and I take the steps two at a time.

It's an old villa. Out front, overgrown lemon trees tumble over each other. A white marble Saleus, god of the ocean, looks gormless in a dry fountain.

I hammer on the front door with the side of my fist. Doubts ping against the periphery of my brain and I grab hold of the fire again. Use the doubts as kindling.

No love. No fear.

Was my whole life a test, Clementine? To see if I could get to this point, like the goddess Thea, free of love and fear? Because I've finally made it. I'm finally free.

The door swings open, and Commodore Price's eyes widen.

"Back again," he says.

Behind him, I can see the faint shapes of a home. A worn couch. A hearth crackling. Despite the grand exterior, it's spartan inside. Even Providence's wealthiest, I suppose, can't live the way anyone did back in Valonia.

I don't see Wes. This is a relief, I think.

"What game are you playing?" he asks.

Another piece of kindling, *whoosh*. I ball my hands at my sides.

"There's a cove a week's sail north of here," I say without preamble. "You can only get in at low tide, and it's hard to spot from the ocean. But if you head due east from Tanager Rock, you'll find it."

"Okay . . . ?" Commodore Price says.

"Clementine will be there on the first day of autumn," I say. "Every year, she meets with some of the other pirate captains to broker alliances."

"The first day of autumn is five weeks away," Price says.

"I know," I say. "So maybe you want to start making a plan."

He blinks like he's trying to collect himself. "Is this some sort of trap?"

"I saved you from Clementine once before," I say. "You don't believe me now?"

"Why would you do this?" he says. "Why *should* I believe you?"

He knows the lesson. He knows how stupid it is to trust anyone.

When I don't answer, he adds, "You'd really tell me how to track down your own mother?"

Are you my daughter or not? she asks, and the fire inside me answers: *Not.*

"Go after her or don't," I say. "Not my problem. But now you know."

I turn to go and he reaches for me, like he's going to grab my wrist, but before he can, I'm pulling out the knife and holding it in front of me. He recoils.

Commodore Price's eyes search me up and down. It makes my skin itch. I can tell he wants to ask me more questions; he doesn't understand what I'm doing here, just like he didn't understand why I freed him when he was stuck on *Asterope's Revenge*.

"Hey," a voice says from farther inside the house. *Oh, no.* "For dinner, would you—"

Wes stops behind his father.

My heart thuds against my ribs.

He's clean now, and more familiar without all the blood. His hair is wet, like he just bathed, but for a minute, all I can see is Wes the way he looked when we swam along the shore in front of our houses. When he agreed to race me even though I always won. When the stars came out and he asked me to name the constellations for him.

I raise the knife higher.

"Needed to steal something else?" Wes asks.

I don't want to answer him—don't even want to look at him—so I keep my attention fixed on Commodore Price. "I know you think this is some sort of trap, but I'm telling you, she'll be there. If you don't catch her, she'll probably just catch you again. And next time, she'll kill you herself."

Both Prices look confused.

"Sir?" Wes says, his voice a little too quiet, and I am suddenly reminded that of course Wes calls his father *Sir*, because they have a forced and formal sort of love. It's one of a thousand things I knew about Wes that stopped being useful when

Clementine took me away. "Can you check the kitchen? I think the soup might be boiling over."

"If that's—"

"Please," Wes says, strained.

Commodore Price, tending his own soup. How times have changed.

The commodore's eyes flick between us, land on my knife, but he nods and backs away, disappearing into the house.

I consider telling him to come back. I consider running. I don't want to be alone with Wes.

"What are you doing here?" he says.

"Telling your father how to find my mother."

"Can I ask why?"

"No," I say.

We watch each other warily for a long time; longer than we should.

"You should let me fix your bandage," he says finally. "You did a terrible job."

"What game are you playing?" Once the question is out of my mouth, I realize it's the same one Commodore Price asked me. The same trite little nothing question one suspicious stranger asks another.

"What game are *you* playing? Why are you here? Not just in Providence, but here, in my shop and at my house?"

"It has nothing to do with you," I say.

He purses his lips, then says, "Wait here."

I think about refusing that too, but before I can make up my mind, he's back, holding a cloth bag.

"What's that?"

"Take it," he says.

I do. When I look inside, I see a loaf of bread. A book of matches. "What's this supposed to be?" I ask. "I don't want it." My stomach betrays me, growling. I keep holding the bag out defiantly, waiting for him to take it back.

He folds his arms across his chest. "My father told me you saved his life."

"I wasn't saving him," I say. "I was just spiting Clementine."

"Oh."

"Take your charity back. I don't want it."

"We're not going to eat it," he says. "We have a fresh loaf. How did you really get here?"

"I swam. I already told you."

"Yes, from a whaling ship. But no whaling ships have gone by in the past week."

I lift my chin. "We were three miles offshore."

When he frowns, his eyebrows pull together.

"You don't believe me," I say. Of course he doesn't.

"I believe you," he says. "It's just, usually people don't do three-mile ocean swims when everything is going well."

"As always, you are an astute observer of the human condition."

"Just eat the bread," he says, sounding tired.

"No."

"You seem like you're trying to prove something, but I don't know what it is."

I scowl at him.

"Do you have somewhere safe to go?" he asks.

"I don't need your help. I said *no*." Now that I've found the word, I can't stop using it. It's luxurious. I've spent so long trying to please people that I have seventeen years' worth of unused *no*'s to spend.

"Thea . . ." he says.

I take a step back.

He doesn't try to follow me, so I take another.

For a minute, I just watch him—all limned in hearth-light, warm and golden, but I don't trust golden boys anymore. I don't trust anyone at all.

I run.

Never again will I allow myself to be in a situation where I'm weak. If I'm alone, I'm the strong one by default.

I slow my pace and look at the bag again. The bread; the matches. I think about leaving them in the dirt, but I'm so, *so* hungry. Just this once, I'll take the charity. As long as I don't do it again.

I wrap my arms around my still-chilled body and gaze up at the endless unfurling of trees. That's when it really hits me, in the quiet, what I just did. Turned Clementine over to Commodore Price. Even if Clementine would've forgiven me for running away, she wouldn't forgive me for this. She might respect me for it, but she wouldn't forgive me. And that's a good thing. I'm going to burn all my bridges until no one can reach me. And that means leaving behind Providence and going somewhere new. Somewhere Clementine can't find me, Wes can't find me, Bauer can't find me.

Alone. I need to be alone.

If Clementine didn't want me to choose my own safety over my family's, she should've named me something else. Libera, maybe. But no: She named me Thea. After the goddess of self-ish, rational detachment. The goddess of not needing anyone. The goddess of being alone.

I step into the forest and don't let myself look back.

PART TWO

THE MYTH OF THEA

THEN AND NOW AND THEN

Then and now and then, twelve gods were birthed by the cosmos.

Each of the twelve wanted to be the most powerful, so they fought over who would rule which domain.

"I shall rule all of nature!" Saleus, the oldest, declared.

His brother, jealous Telamon, said, "That is too much."

"Then I shall take all the seas," Saleus said.

"I will take skies and storms," Telamon countered.

And so it went. Ten brothers parceled up the world until it was the turn of the two sisters, Thea and Libera. Crafty Thea realized there was nothing in nature left to take; seas, skies, plants, animals—all were gone. But still, she hungered to be powerful. She could, she realized, take a slice of each god's domain if she understood it better than he did.

"I shall take cleverness," Thea said. "Rationality, reason, and intellect."

"She can't!" jealous Telamon bellowed. "A goddess cannot claim the mind."

"A bargain, then," crafty Thea said. "We fight by blade.

Whoever draws first blood of the other will claim domain of the mind."

Telamon, convinced no goddess could best him, agreed.

But Thea had been watching the gods carefully as they chose their domains. She saw how Telamon gazed at her sister, Libera, with desire. So when Thea and Telamon raised their blades, Thea did not first strike Telamon. Instead, she spun and sliced Libera's arm.

Telamon cried out and dropped his blade. He rushed to Libera's aid. Thea easily pierced his chest, and in an instant, the battle was won.

"You tricked me!" Telamon shouted as his immortal flesh began to heal.

"I am already the ruler of cleverness," Thea said. "From love and fear comes all weakness; I have neither, so I have no weakness. There is nothing to cloud my rationality; nothing to impede my strength."

So while the other gods continued to bicker, the goddess Thea descended, knowing that it did not matter which domains they chose; with her unflinching mind, she was the most powerful of the gods.

Chapter Nine

Now

Seventeen years old

Galatean Mountains, east of Providence

I walk for two days through the forest, climbing between trees and over rocks and through brambles. I don't know where I'm heading, exactly, other than away from Providence. By the end of the second day, both my socks have holes in the heels and my feet are bleeding in about five places. Fortunately, my forehead finally scabbed over.

Wes's bread is long gone; I regret eating it, but I also regret not accepting more. When I smell smoke, I follow my nose to another settlement. It's no bigger than Providence. People give me the same concerned, vaguely affronted looks I got back down the mountain, but at least here, no one is familiar.

My stomach has been hardening into a progressively tighter knot. Following the creek kept me from getting too thirsty, but if I don't figure out a more sustainable food situation soon, I'm in trouble.

I make myself a home out of sight of civilization. The trees are gnarled, many-limbed oaks, the kind whose trunks zig parallel to the ground before zagging vertical again. They're furred with lichen and draped with vines. I choose a rock with a cozy nook underneath and start to make my fire.

It's my fourth fire now. I've done one every night, and another on the second morning because I was so cold I couldn't move my toes. The first fire took me three matches. But I got better since then, and I'm learning which sticks burn well and which moss will just smoke. The book has only fourteen more matches, and I'm nervous about using them up. I'm nervous about using them at all, actually—whenever I strike one, I wince, feeling the tug of the long tether that leads me back to Wes.

I tuck myself underneath the rock. The empty bag, I roll up to use as a pillow. Just to be safe, I take out Clementine's knife. I sleep with it in one hand.

The exhaustion of walking should put me right to sleep, but it never works. I can't stop running through imaginary conversations with Clementine.

Where did you go? she shouts. *Why did you leave?*

Remember that boy from Tanager Rock? I try to say. *Did you ever meet the innkeepers' son? I thought I loved—*

There's no way to begin the story, so my mind skips over that part. Jumps past the rocky explanation and gets to the bit where Clementine looks at me, confused, angry.

Why didn't I scream? That's what Clementine would ask me, if I told her. *Why didn't you put your thumbs in his eyes? Fight him? Hurt him?*

I don't know, Clementine. I'm sorry.

But who could've screamed? He wasn't a stranger. He was Bauer. He was supposed to be a future, not an ending.

I don't mean to hedge. About Bauer. About what he did to me. I just hate all the words at my disposal. *Took advantage of me?* It makes it sound like we were playing a board game. *Raped?* It makes me feel like war-scorched land.

Bauer's not evil, I don't think. That's the worst part. If he'd done this with malice, it would make it easier to hate him. But he didn't have malice; he just never thought. The world never made him.

I wonder, if I ever make it out from under this lovely, solid rock, if Bauer might see me in ten years' time. Maybe in a harbor somewhere. He'll be with the crew of his whaling ship— he'll be a harpooneer by then—and striding down the dock when I step off a ship of my own. He won't recognize me, not at first, but I will recognize him. Instantly.

I will feel hands claiming my body. A mouth too hot and too rough against my neck. I will want to yell, revolt, avenge. Will want to make him feel as small and powerless as he made me.

We'll be still. Facing each other on the dock.

And he'll smile.

When I find my crew again, they'll ask me, *Thea, who was he?*

No one, I'll say. *He's no one.*

And the whalers, once they stride out of earshot, jostling each other and laughing, they'll say, *Bauer, who was she?*

He'll smile that syrupy, lazy smile. *Just a girl I once fucked.*

I bet, for a moment, he'll feel good about himself. And then he'll forget again.

But I won't forget him for the rest of my life.

CHAPTER TEN

THEN

SIXTEEN YEARS OLD

TANAGER ROCK

I first met Bauer when I was sixteen, just a few days after my birthday. People packed the pebbled walkway around the Tanager Rock harbor. The smell of freshly tanned leather acidified the breeze. Somewhere in the distance, the clouds were getting blacker, fatter, and lower, but no one was paying much attention when there was drink to be drunk.

When Clementine and I first set sail, I assumed we'd only be on the water for a few days. A month, maybe. I missed solid ground. I missed being among people whose lives didn't revolve around Clementine. But we only went to the continent to steal: food, water, sails, wood, oil. And the only land where I was free to wander was this land, Tanager Rock. It was an island about a mile wide, thrown just northwest of the settlements where the surviving Valonians—a thousand in total, as far as I knew—had landed.

Tanager Rock was lush, wooded, covered in wildflowers and

shaggy trees. There were birds, so many birds, and for the last mile as we approached the docks, we could hear the chirruping of tanagers.

This was a place for pirates to congregate, sell stolen goods, and repair their ships. There was no farming, no mining, none of the things settlers on the continent were trying to do to survive. We survived off them like parasites. None of the other pirates seemed to care that the more we succeeded at stealing from the settlements, the more they shrunk. We'd kill our hosts and then have no blood left to drink.

For two years, I'd lived on *Asterope's Revenge*. I'd gotten better at schooling my hysterical outbursts of such unsavory emotions as *sadness*. By then, I disappointed Clementine less, but she was also paying less attention, which meant I had fewer opportunities to let her down.

I still hadn't proved myself ready to captain a ship.

To everyone but Clementine, it was obvious: I was a terrible pirate, but I threw myself into the sailing, if not the pillaging aspect of things. I did what the mates told me to do; I kept my head down. By candlelight, I read books on whales, ships, human bodies. Sometimes, I could go a whole day without saying anything other than "Yes, ma'am."

Livia caught my arm while I was still waiting on the edge of the crowd. "Did you see Clementine leave?"

"No. Why?"

"She seemed . . . off."

I frowned. I didn't like the thought that someone else could

track Clementine's moods better than I could. "I'm sure she's fine."
To change the subject, I asked, "Want to go into the market?"

"I have exactly no money on hand," Livia said. "I suppose we'll have to engage in some light thievery."

"Brilliant! I've always dreamed of getting my fingers chopped off."

Livia dropped my arm and stepped into the crowd. I hurried to match her pace, trying to keep her in view; her black hair, pulled into a bun at the nape of her neck, bobbed ahead.

The street was lined with as many unfamiliar faces as familiar ones. Some women were dressed like Livia and me, in boots and bandanas, but others wore dresses, red on their lips. One woman bent to retrieve something under the shade of a canopy, and I watched the blue and white stripes of her skirt crinkle along smart pleats. When she stood, cheeks flushed, she held a tortoiseshell guitar pick between her thumb and forefinger.

I didn't realize I was staring until Livia said, "Do you play anything? I don't know how I've never asked."

"What?"

Livia nodded to the booth, where string instruments hung from hooks. The woman caught us looking and waved us over.

"You know," Livia said, "I bought Cadmus a mandolin on his eighteenth birthday. He was so bad at playing, it went *mysteriously* missing a week later."

Cadmus was Livia's younger brother. He sailed with Clementine too, and sometimes made me laugh with jokes under his breath about our crewmates. They were both older than me, but still in their early twenties, so if I were to consider anyone on *Asterope* friends, it would be the two of them.

"Want to go look?" I asked. "Maybe you inherited the musical genes."

"I think instruments fall into the category of things I can't afford," Livia said. "I'm going to the booth with the books. Maybe they have philosophy."

I walked to the music stall alone. The woman beamed. A dust-colored curl sprang from beneath her wide hat, which was tied with a sash under her chin.

"Is that a lyre?" I asked, pointing.

"Yes! Do you play?"

I shook my head, but the woman was already picking the lyre off the hook, her back turned. "Not really," I said. "My father did."

The woman plucked a few strings, smiling, then passed me the instrument. It was lighter than I expected—I hadn't held one since my father died. I caught one of the strings between my thumb and nail. It twanged.

"Did you make all these?"

"No. My husband's work." She rose on her toes to look over my head. "He's off, oh, somewhere."

A pang of loss. The version of this woman I was assembling in my head was an independent artisan, boldly carting her wares alone.

I dragged my thumb across the strings. "Do sailors of ill repute buy many instruments?"

She laughed. "More than you'd expect, actually. I grew up here, so the ill repute doesn't bother me."

"I didn't know anyone grew up on Tanager Rock."

"I'm Hanna," the woman said. "My parents run the inn. The Bauers?"

I shook my head. We'd stayed at the inn before, but I didn't recognize Hanna, or the name.

A cold wind whipped past. Hanna pressed her hands against her skirt to keep it from blowing. We both glanced out at the horizon, just for a moment. The clouds were getting closer.

"What's your name?" Hanna asked.

"Thea."

"Oh! Then the lyre suits you."

I handed it back to her, suddenly ashamed that I didn't know how to play. "My parents loved the Classical myths."

"Who doesn't?" Hanna said. She smiled back at me, and warmth ballooned in my stomach. How long had it been since I'd talked to someone who wasn't a pirate? Who didn't know Clementine?

Another gust of wind. I fought a shiver.

Hanna wrapped her arms around the lyre, rising on her toes again. "I wish I knew where my—oh, there."

A moment later, a man stepped into the booth. He wore plain trousers and a white shirt, the top button undone. His jaw was covered in something that might've been stubble, but his hair was honey blond, the same shade as his skin, too fair to know for sure. I couldn't tell whether his curls were tousled because of the wind or because he thought he looked good that way.

He took the lyre out of Hanna's hands. "I don't like the speed those clouds are moving. Let's get all this inside."

I called him a man when I first saw him, but he couldn't have been much older than I was. "Are you Hanna's husband?"

He spun, like he hadn't seen me before, and when he did, he smiled. "Her husband isn't half as good-looking as I am."

Hanna snatched the lyre back again. "Gideon isn't half as much an ass as you are." To me, she said, "This is my brother. A brother who, if he loved me, would help carry all these instruments. Oh, damn."

A plunk of rain against the canopy. The crowd on the street hurried for cover.

"Do you need help?" I asked.

"Oh, would you?" Hanna said. "You're wonderful. The crates are over there."

"If Gideon is such a good man," the brother said, "where is he?" When he walked past Hanna, violin case in hand, he bumped his hip to hers. It could've been an accident. Probably not. Not having siblings of my own, I watched their movements like a scientist.

"Maybe he thought my loving family would be willing to help," Hanna said. "Like my new friend Thea." When she walked by her brother to retrieve a mandolin, she bumped him even harder.

By the time we got all the instruments in their cases and all the cases in their crates, the rain was falling in earnest. I shared a crate with Hanna while her brother took the other. We hurried down the deserted path to the inn.

Even from outside, I could tell the inn was full to bursting, busy with noise and light and smoke. Hanna led the way—"Excuse me, pardon, excuse me"—to an unobtrusive side hall. When I finally set down the crate, my hands were marked with angry red lines.

"For what it's worth," Hanna's brother said, "I saw Gideon at the bar with an empty pint. But tell me again how charming he is."

Hanna let out a breath and straightened her hat. "Stay away from my brother, Thea. He's a meddling little bastard." She marched back into the crowded room.

When I was alone with the meddling little bastard, he leaned against the wall. His smile was lazy, syrup slow. "So. You're Thea?"

"I'm Thea. What's your name?"

"Call me Bauer," he said. "Do you know where your people are?"

"My people?"

"Presumably, you didn't row here from the continent in a dinghy made for one. But if you did, my congratulations on your arm strength."

I had no idea where Livia went when the rain started. And as for Clementine—I hadn't seen her since we docked. I shook my head. "I don't know where they are."

Wind rattled the windows. Bauer tilted his head. "By the

sound of it, you might want to wait until the weather clears to find them. Come on, I'll get you something to drink."

So I was separated from Clementine and the crew for a few hours. I couldn't pretend to be disappointed.

I followed Bauer to the bar, where men crammed on every seat and filled the spaces in between. Bauer stepped around them and walked behind the bar, back to the sink and the taps and the glasses. I paused.

"Come on," he said. That slow smile. "Nothing to be scared of." He held out his hand.

I took it, and he pulled me after him.

Oh.

My hand felt warm. All of me felt warm.

That was interesting.

Standing behind the bar made me feel like an adult. Not one of the crowd, but someone in charge. I scanned the room. A few familiar pirates, but none from Clementine's crew. At the other end of the bar, I saw, but couldn't hear, Hanna hissing at a pink-cheeked man who wasn't half as attractive as she was.

"Where are your parents?" I asked.

"Afraid you'll get in trouble?"

"No," I said. *Yes.*

"In the kitchen, probably," he said. "Or serving customers. Don't worry. Didn't I tell you there was nothing to be scared of?"

He motioned for me to sit on the back counter, and I did, swinging my legs and watching the chaos. As he filled pints and accepted coins—on Tanager Rock, it seemed they accepted a wide variety of coins—I watched the door. Whenever it opened, it let in a blast of frigid air. Then everyone yelled, and the newcomer slammed the door shut again and said, "Sorry, sorry!" The newcomer was never Livia, or Cadmus, or Clementine. But I kept watching.

When Bauer got through the backlog of drinkless drinkers, he turned to face me, resting his elbows behind him on the bar. The flickering light, golden as his skin and his curls, suited him. "So if you didn't row here in a dinghy, what's your ship?"

"*Asterope's Revenge*," I said.

He whistled. "You sail with Clementine Fowler? I hear she's a piece of work."

"I'm her daughter." Bauer's eyebrows lifted, so I hurried to add, "And you're right. She's a piece of work."

He laughed. It was smooth, like his smile. "I didn't realize I was in the company of a pirate-queen-in-waiting."

"Oh." I didn't know if he meant it as a compliment or not. "I'm hardly a pirate. It's mostly Clementine."

"You call your mother Clementine?"

I glanced at the door again. "She thought it made more sense once we started sailing. Didn't see the point in reminding the rest of the crew I was her daughter every time I spoke to her."

A man tapped a coin against the bar impatiently. Bauer held up his hand to me as he poured a drink.

When he turned back, I said, "Crowded tonight."

"It's not so bad," he said. "Is it true Clementine was from some fancy Valonian family?"

"Fancy? I don't know about that."

Bauer grinned. "Come on. I bet you were fancy. Big skirts? Learning how to ballroom dance at school?"

"Hardly," I said. "Clementine sent me to an all-boys school." Bauer kept grinning like I was making a joke. And it did sound ridiculous, I supposed. I tried to change the subject again. "Do you like working for your parents?"

"Nah," Bauer said. "So, how big is Clementine's crew?"

"Twenty-four. Why?"

"Is it true she stole her ship?"

"Yes." When I didn't say anything else, he filled up another pint with something—beer or ale or cider, how would I know?—and handed it to me. I didn't really want it, but he was being so generous that I wasn't sure how to say no. I took a sip. It tasted like lemons.

"This is all my life has ever been," he said. "Working the inn. Hearing about adventures I can't go on." A pause. "Your life must be a lot more exciting."

It was an invitation to say more. To tell the whole bloody tale of the famous Clementine Fowler and *Asterope's Revenge*. From how many ships had she stolen? How many people had she killed for not surrendering? I'd gotten inured to the idea of my mother as a killer. The person who made my life also took lives from other people. Often. It was just the way of things. Didn't mean I wanted to talk about it. Like accepting the drink, I didn't know how to say no without offending him.

"Well," I said. I took another sip. Still bad. "When I was fourteen, my father died."

"How?"

I swallowed. "The earthquakes. Before Mount Telamon erupted. My parents knew it was coming too, but nobody believed them."

Bauer took a slow sip of his drink. He said nothing, just watched me talk.

"Anyway, Clementine got really angry when he died. Started talking about how the world would never listen to us and we had to protect ourselves. She's kind of like Thea in the Classical myths—that's why she named me Thea. She's the only goddess who can fight the male gods. You've read the old myths?"

Bauer looked blankly at me. In the distance, someone started to play the piano. The notes plunked slowly, gently through the air.

"Oh," I said. My cheeks felt hot. I knew I was starting to ramble. "Well, Clementine was always sort of . . . independent. She doesn't like being told who to be." Bauer stared at me intently, and I shifted under the attention. I looked down at the foam drifting on top of my glass. "Anyway. We got on *Asterope's Revenge* and never looked back. I haven't seen anyone from my old life since."

Except Wes.

But I wished I didn't have to count that.

"Wow," Bauer said. A long pause. His eyes ran the length of me. "I'm sorry."

"Don't be," I said. Guilt hit me right away—I was always telling people that my father's death and everything that followed was nothing to worry about, that I was fine, but I wasn't fine. I missed him every day. And I missed my life. "Everyone lost someone during the eruption."

"No," Bauer said. "I mean, yes, I'm sorry about your father. But I meant, I'm sorry Clementine took you from your home just like that."

I didn't know how to respond. *Thank you? You're right?*

"Do you like living on the ship?" Bauer asked.

I shrugged. "It's all right. I like seeing all the animals. Birds and orcas and porpoises."

"I love whales," Bauer said. It was so earnest, so intent. Warmth filled my stomach.

"I see lots of whales. You notice animals more when you're not surrounded by so many people. And there's lots of time to read."

"It sounds lonely," he said.

How could Bauer see me so plainly after a matter of hours when Clementine, sixteen years after giving birth to me, still hardly knew me? Bauer cut me bare. I liked it. I liked him.

My cheeks grew warm again and I motioned to the door, searching for a change of subject. "I can't believe how bad this storm is."

"I'll protect you," Bauer said wryly. His smile twisted at the corner.

"Very funny." I leaned back on the counter. "Do you like living here?"

"Here? What were you saying about *very funny?*"

I grinned, but before I could respond, the door—the

door I left unwatched for a moment too long—swung open. Clementine threw herself inside. The chorus of yells at the wind died quickly; Clementine didn't say *Sorry, sorry*. It was like she sensed I'd managed to think about something other than her for thirty seconds and couldn't stand the betrayal.

I slid off the counter. "I have to go."

Bauer didn't try to stop me. I squeezed around the bar and started threading my way to Clementine, but at the last minute, I turned back. Bauer was wiping down a glass, the shards of lantern light turning it prismatic in his hands.

"You said I could call you Bauer, but that's your last name, right?"

He looked up at me through his eyelashes.

"What's your first name?"

He set down the glass. *Clink.* "Leo." Syrup smile. "Leo Bauer."

Before we sailed the next day, I hunted around the inn for Bauer. *Leo Bauer.*

I was surprised by how much I wanted to see him again. But oh, I did. I was hungry not just for his attention, his smile, but for the way I felt around him. Like I mattered. Like I was more than a pirate.

It was mid-morning, cool but bright, when I found him. He was behind the inn, feeding a pen of goats. As he threw chunks of stale bread, watching the goats jump, he laughed with his whole body.

"Thea!" Bauer said when he saw me. There was no moment of pretending we'd never met. No waiting to see if I'd pretend. He was confident—I liked it. "Sleep well?"

I could smell cinnamon on his breath, like spicy tea.

"Very," I said. "You?"

His smile had mischief. "I had fascinating dreams."

"Oh?"

"But it's even lovelier to talk to you in person."

My face burned. "Well," I said, "I missed your scintillating conversation."

"I'm honored," he said. "We never got to finish it."

I wasn't sure that was true, but I felt flattered to be treated this way—important, like an old friend—so I didn't correct him.

"I'm busy doing things for my parents today," Bauer said. "But can I show you something?"

I nodded. I only had a few minutes anyway before we were meant to disembark.

He took my hand. Laced his fingers through mine. No hesitation. It was so unassuming, the warmth of his palm. Like there was no reason not to hold hands.

He pulled me back inside, past the bar, down a hallway. I followed him into a closet, soap-scented and dim.

"I went out to the beach this morning to get some air," he said. "I found this. It's a whale rib." He lifted a bone, chalk white and curved and as long as I was tall. "I'm not sure what kind of whale."

I brushed the surface with a finger. "Oh," I said. "Oh, it's beautiful. Why'd you bring it back here?"

He laughed. "You said you liked whales."

On the rib, our hands were staggered. Mine, his, mine, his. His thumb brushed the underside of my wrist.

"How long are you staying?" he asked.

"Not long. Clementine has . . . plans."

"I still can't believe you're Clementine Fowler's daughter," he said.

"Is that supposed to be an insult?"

"Of course not. You're too sweet to be a pirate."

I was going to protest—tell him I wasn't sweet, didn't want to be told I was—but Bauer tugged the rib, pulling me closer.

He kissed me quickly, like maybe he hadn't expected to do it. His mouth was hot. His hands, closing on top of mine on the whale rib, were calloused. My lips parted.

He stopped kissing me just as fast. Then he smiled and stepped away.

"Come back to Tanager Rock soon," he said.

That was my first kiss. I hadn't even thought of kissing anyone since I left Valonia.

I bent to set down the rib. When I stood up again, Bauer was gone.

I took the path to the harbor alone, my arms wrapped around my torso and my hands under my armpits.

Clementine was building a fleet. She wanted me to learn how to be a captain. She wanted me to *prove myself.*

But for the first time, I had a secret. I had a window into a world that didn't belong to Clementine: Bauer. I felt like more of a child and more of an adult than ever.

I saw my future like a tree with two branches: on one, a world where Clementine trusted me; on the other, a world where people might think I was not like Clementine and better for it. I had glimpsed, with Bauer, a peek into the new. A peek into the possible.

This was an inflection point.

This was where everything would change.

Chapter Eleven

Now

Seventeen years old

Takvik

I wake up when a bee lands on my arm.

I startle, and the bee takes off. The idea hits me fast. Scrambling to my feet, I kick past the remains of my campfire and follow the bee. I lose it, of course—it's a bee in a forest, and I'm a lumbering, sleepy human—but it only takes a few minutes of standing among the wildflowers to find another, and then another. There's a fig tree nearby, and in the shade of its branches is a box, about as long as my arm and crawling with vines. It looks like no one's touched it in years. The bees buzz past me, totally unconcerned, before politely waiting their turn to climb inside the box. They're the sleek, dutiful kind, feet all dusted with pollen and glowing golden in the dawn light. We had a beehive like this in our yard in Valonia. My father harvested the honey twice a summer, and he even let me hold the frames once.

If I'm going to get food, I'm going to need money. The half-formed plan in my head seems as good as any.

It takes me the whole day—and about two dozen bee stings—to figure out how to do it. I steal a bucket from the nearby settlement. Collect as much of the smoky moss as possible. Use up another three of my matches. I put my holey socks on my hands, not that they do much good, and lift out the first frame. I take a quick breath. My father did this every summer. So can I. The frame is white with thick, sealed wax. Full of eggs? I don't think so, but I'm not entirely sure what to look for. When I shake away the bees—another sting. I wince. But by the time the sun is setting, Clementine's knife is covered in sticky honey and my bucket is full of severed comb. I don't know how much the bees need to survive, or if someone might show up to reclaim the hive, so I take two frames' worth but leave the rest. The next morning, I make my way to a bakery in the middle of the settlement. I pass a group of young mothers who recoil when they see—or smell—me. I scowl at them, but their fear gives me a little thrill. I am the forest-born bee woman. Tremble, all who know me.

When I open the bakery door, the baker says something in a language I don't understand.

"Um . . . What?"

"No money, no bread," he says in Astorian.

I've never been outside Astoria before. I suppose I finally reached the edge somewhere in the mountains. I feel a rush of adrenaline at the thought of *elsewhere*.

"I was actually hoping for a trade," I say, holding up my bucket.

Twenty minutes later, I'm leaving the bakery with two loaves of bread, a block of cheese, a glass jar of my honey. The baker also gives me three dirty copper chips. They're not Astorian coins, but who cares? In this town, they buy bread. The baker told me to come back with more honey if I could find it, and rather pointedly suggested I take a bath first.

I clutch the bag of food to my chest. The bread is hot against my heart. I'm smiling like an idiot.

I'm keeping myself alive.

It feels so good.

I've always liked sunrises, but now that I hate sleep, I start to love them with fanatical fervor. Sleep is fractured and terrifying, full of vivid half-dreams and cold sweat.

You betrayed Clementine.

You disappointed Clementine.

You will never, ever be Clementine.

But then I watch the platinum sun, beams of warmth cutting the mist, blackening the trees in their way and revealing all the subtle textures of bark, leaf, grass lost in the darkness. The morning horizon still can't save me, but it's another day, and with it comes another chance to save myself.

This is a thing I've learned about surviving. There never comes a day when you're done doing it. You just have to keep choosing, over and over again, to watch this brand-new sun, to find a beehive, to eat your bread, to survive.

The settlement, I've learned, is called Takvik. They fashion

themselves as a waypoint between the coastal settlements—
Providence, Silver Creek, Fairshore—and the river settlements
on the other side of the mountains. I don't know what's beyond
those settlements. Another coast, maybe. Or maybe fields,
plains, steppes, tundra. Could be anything. From overheard
snippets of conversation, I gather that Takvik is populated by
both Astorians and people from beyond the mountains.

On my third trip into town, a pair of men beat me to the
baker's counter, and I hear them talking about how they're
going to the river settlements, and that it's their fourth trip
across the Galatean Mountains.

I'm feeling twitchy as I wait with my bucket of honeycomb.
There are more hives, dozens of them, out in the woods. They
all have the air of being forgotten about, but I'm still afraid to
take more than a little bit at a time.

I caught a glimpse of myself in the window of one of the
shops on the way here, and I don't look good. My hair is
the color and texture of frayed rope—a matted blond that
won't ever come untangled. I'm covered with bee stings, and
I'm hoping the window glass was warped and my face isn't
swelling as badly as it looked.

One of the men in front of me says *pirate* and I go still.

How many days has it been since I left Providence? Seven?
Ten? Something like that.

It's nine.

Even to myself, I pretend I don't know. I pretend I don't see
the looming numbers flashing on the backs of my eyelids every

morning: *TWENTY-EIGHT DAYS UNTIL COMMODORE PRICE FINDS CLEMENTINE.*

So what if Commodore Price finds Clementine? That's what I wanted. So what if I never talk to her again? I'm certainly not going to run back to Providence just so I can see her face. Just so I can get her validation, recognition, love, hatred, *anything*.

I don't care.

I've been coming up with tricks to reassure myself it was the right—the *strong*—thing to do, telling Commodore Price about her. I make myself repeat things she said to me: *Are you my daughter or not? Be quiet. Get angry!* I force myself to dig my nails into the oozing flesh of memory and hold it in my hands until the fire lights up my stomach again. Until my anger burns away my shame.

But all it takes is one stray thought, one stray word, and I'm scared all over again. Scared Clementine is captured or dead. Scared it's my fault.

Pirate.

"—pirates got half the shipment," the man is saying.

"Hardly worth our time," the other says, "but we wanted to head home before the weather rolled in."

"We expecting bad weather?" the baker asks.

"Count on it," the first man says.

"As long as it's not bad enough to kill me." The baker hands over a loaf of bread and a jar of honey. My honey. I feel a little bubble of pride.

"Cheers," the second man says.

The two traders flinch when they see me. I keep my face impassive.

"You know," the baker says as I set my bucket on his counter, "the town is talking about you."

"I am a beauty of some renown," I say. I poke the bucket. "How much can I get for this?"

He fixes me with a hard look. I think he means it to be *knowing,* but he can't know anything about me. I'm an enigma. I'm the bee woman.

"Ten petrels," he says.

"It was twelve last time."

"Well, you've saturated the market." A pause. Then he asks, "Do you want a job?"

"No. Why would I want a job?" I have a job. Collecting honey and not dying.

"The town's talking," he says again. "One of the kids says you've been living in the woods."

My hand goes automatically to the knife at my hip. It shouldn't be a surprise that someone would think I was living in the woods—I have about half of the woods stuck to my hair—but I hate the thought that someone might've followed me back to my shelter. Might've watched me sleep. Seen me eat.

"There's a spare closet at the back," the baker says. "I don't really need an assistant, but, I don't know, you can stay for free and eat all the stale bread you want."

I size him up. He's about my height, stocky. Pinkish white

skin and a brown beard. I'd guess he's twenty-five. He's covered with flour and his cheeks are flushed, maybe from being near the oven, or maybe just because that's how he looks. There is nothing about him that screams *untrustworthy,* except for the fact that he's a human being.

"Pass," I say. "But I'll keep bringing you honey."

"I can only sell so much honey."

"Then I'll take it somewhere else."

"Can I do anything for you?" he asks.

"Actually," I say, because there *is* something that's been bothering me, "do you know where I can buy some flint?"

It takes me a few tries to learn the trick with the flint, just like it did with the matches, just like it did with the hives. But eventually, I'm watching my first self-made, self-earned fire bloom and crackle. I paid for this flint. Me.

From my pocket, I pull Wes's matchbook. The very last match still sits in place, expectant. I know I should save it for an emergency, but I don't. I toss it in my baby fire and watch it light. Even though I might not have made it this far without Wes's gift, in this moment, I feel free of it. Like I don't owe anyone anything. The only person keeping Thea alive is Thea. The tether between Wes and me snaps, and it feels so good, I start to cry.

I sit down hard under the edge of my rock. The ground is damp. I know every contour of this clearing: the two pines that brush together, *whisk whisk,* and sound like footsteps. The boulder that looks like a bear at night.

For a minute, I let myself cry, about everything and nothing, and then I scrub my eyes with the heels of my hands. It's lunchtime. I like lunchtime.

I lay the bread out carefully. You have to take everything slowly when you have too much time in your day. Otherwise, the minutes start to feel overwhelming, inexhaustible. So I polish Clementine's knife on the hem of my shirt—probably getting it dirtier in the process—and cut a careful, even chunk of bread. A thin slice of cheese. I stick the blade in my jar of honey and drizzle it across the bread, my hands, everything, and then I lick it clean.

I eat slowly, chewing every bite until the bread starts to dissolve in my mouth. The knife, I keep on my lap. I took it because it made me feel strong and fierce in the way that Clementine is strong and fierce. I took it as a weapon. But now I use it for a different kind of strength. This quintessentially domestic act: cutting my food to nourish my body to keep on living.

What if I worked at the bakery?

I won't. I tell myself I won't, and once I've done that, I let my mind play with the idea. Not as a real consideration. Just a . . . thought experiment.

I think I'd cut my hair. It's too knotted to fix. I'd cut my hair, cute and short, and tuck it behind my ears, and I'd wear an apron covered in flour. My first few loaves would be awful, but I'd get better, and then I'd start experimenting. A pair of traders would trek through with a crate of dried vanilla beans, and I'd smell them and say, "Reminds me of the bakery in Valonia!" And they'd say, "You from Valonia? Us too!" I'd spend all night in the kitchen, fiddling with the vanilla and honey, and when the baker woke up in the morning, he'd say, "Thea! Didn't you sleep?" I'd tell him no—I had to perfect my nautilus roll recipe, but I'd finally done it, made them just like the bakery back in Valonia a million years ago. He'd take a bite, close his eyes, and smile.

There's a tight knot in my throat as I cut another thin, precise slice of bread.

Or.

I'd cut my hair, and when I looked in the mirror, my reflection would stare back at me, sunken-eyed, still too familiar. *Think that's enough to become a new person? You're not fooling anyone.* My first few loaves would be awful, and the ones after that too, and the baker would say, "Didn't anyone ever teach you how to do anything right?" A pair of traders would trek through with a crate of dried vanilla beans, and tears would spring unbidden to my eyes. One of the traders, his breath like gin, hot and poisonous, would lean forward and scrape the tears away with his thumb. "Sad little girl," he'd say. "I can make you feel better." I would run, would hide all night, and the baker would throw open my door in the morning and say, "Thea! Didn't you sleep? You think your shitty bread is going to get any better if you don't sleep?" I'd tell him no—I was scared, I wanted to leave, I wanted to run. "Thea," he would say. "You're safe here. You trust me. You're not going anywhere." And then he would press a wet kiss to my forehead, close his eyes, and smile.

When I cut my next slice of bread, I nick my thumb, and I watch the blood well.

Fifteen days since I left Providence. Twenty-two until Clementine goes to the cove to meet the other pirate captains, and Commodore Price goes to intercept her.

There's another count I've been doing in my head.

One, two, three days since I was supposed to get my period.

Coincidence. It's a coincidence.

I go about my day. Fire, breakfast, clean in the river. Lunch, hive, bakery. Fire, dinner, sleep. Ignore everything else. Survive, survive, survive.

When I wake up the next morning, knife tight in my hand, I wake to blood.

I'm so relieved that I start to pant, somewhere between a laugh and a sob. There will be no proof of Bauer. I can still be a child. I don't have to become Clementine, a mother afraid of mothering. I am still—

I press a hand to my mouth.

Breathe.

I clean my underwear in the creek. I'd like to treat myself to a spare set of clothes—I have a jangling little coin pocket by now—but Takvik is too small for clothing shops. At the bakery, I pay for my loaf of bread. It's still hot through the paper sleeve. I can't meet the baker's gaze. I'm still thinking of my waking nightmare, that wet kiss on my forehead.

Before he can say anything, I hurry back to my rock. I decide to take the day off from bee-finding. I curl in my bed of moss and watch the flames and eat slowly.

Another day. Another chance to save myself.

"See, Clementine?" I whisper. "I'm doing it."

But I'm not sure how much longer I can.

I don't want to go back to the bakery. I can no longer look at the baker without imagining his lips on my forehead.

There's a rational part of me that knows how foolish this is. The baker's been nothing but kind. My own mind is the enemy here.

Still.

I can't go back.

Fortunately, I don't have to. I've collected enough coins that I can spend them elsewhere in Takvik. One fewer person whose kindness I'm dependent upon. Now I flit like a ghost between shops, butcher and grocer, anonymous as any mountain traveler if I keep my head down.

And the days keep passing.

A funny thing happens once I start to get my slice of the forest in order. I would've thought that once I had water and food and enough coins for a bee-less day, I would start to relax. Maybe buy a few books. Nap. I don't know. But the less I have to occupy my time, the more the world seems to balloon out in front of me, unfathomably large. Each hour is an abyss, and I have too many of them.

I perfect things that already worked fine. Remake my shelter—branches and boards leaning up against my rock—three times over, even though I end up with no protection from the wind during the remaking. My stockpile of simple foods grows, but as the danger of starvation wanes, my fear of death waxes. I no longer have a concrete danger on which to pin my fears, so the fears latch on to everything. Crunching leaves and cold wind and the globular rain clouds. What's going to kill me today? *Anything, everything.*

In the back of my mind, I start imagining Providence. The wet, earthy air and the metronome of the waves. A forest where the grass was literally greener.

There are dangers there: Clementine, Bauer, Commodore Price, Wes. They'd all look for me there, if they cared to look anywhere. But these trees, this dirt, the rocks that once felt so full of possibility have lost all their magic and gone gray with age. There is nothing for me here but the hours, expanding. How is it possible to be so afraid and so bored at the same time? Maybe the boredom is what I'm afraid of. I am afraid of an unextraordinary life, an unextraordinary death, a long trudge to nothing.

On the third day after this intrusive thought takes root in my brain, I try to remind myself: I left Providence for a reason. It would be more dangerous there.

But maybe that's what I want.

I've been taught that humans are always either strong or weak; winners or losers; Thea or Libera. I imagined that being alone would make me feel strong—a heroine fending for herself, braving the great unknown. But maybe strength is a thing not felt alone. Maybe you can't be strong without making someone else weak.

If I go back to Providence, Wes might try to help me again. But I burned his last match. I don't need him anymore, and I won't owe him anything.

That day, I pack up my food and flint in a new rucksack, one paid for with my honey. Wes's bag, I burn in my breakfast campfire. I have two skins of creek water and Clementine's knife on my hip.

As I go, I touch the trunks of the trees that stood sentinel above me as I slept. There's no one here to laugh at me, but I still feel foolish doing it.

Summer's almost gone, and the air knows—the shadows have chill. Ten days, and summer's gone. Ten days, and it's the first day of autumn, and with it, the autumn armistice, and Commodore Price's chance to catch Clementine at the cove.

A few miles down the mountain, I find a glimmer of Providence in the distance, a speck of gold on the fog-drenched seaside. With each step, I feel my lungs getting a little fuller. Movement feels like remembering. This is more than survival; this is purpose. I try not to worry about how fleeting it is. A two days' walk? Maybe I'll go slow. Try to find more hives along the way. Ration this walk like the last glob of honey in the jar.

A branch breaks nearby. My breath catches, and I lurch back. Through the tangle of trees: cat eyes. They watch me.

"What are you?" I whisper. Bobcat? Cougar? Something I've never seen before? Something no one has ever seen before? It slinks back into the dark edges of the forest, but it's a long time before my heart stops racing.

If I died out here, no one would ever know.

I shiver.

I feel somehow more vulnerable and more capable of armoring my vulnerabilities than ever; I'm critically aware of my fears, but doesn't that help me cover them? It's somehow deeply childish and insidiously grown-up. I'm more of a child and more of an adult than—

Here. Now.

My mind is grappling with the past, but I won't go. There's no use thinking about what's done. I try to tell my body, *I'm here, can't you see?* In the forest. Walking. I have purpose.

Here. Now.

I *won't* worry about the end of the walk. Things are getting better. I'm getting better. Stronger. The fact that I'm going back to Providence is proof of that. The people from my old life don't scare me anymore.

This is an inflection point.

This is where everything changes.

Chapter Twelve

Now

Seventeen years old

Galatean Mountains, east of Providence

It's faster down the mountain than it was going up. By the time the sun sets and I make camp, I'm only a few hours' walk from Providence.

I sleep in the hollow of a tree. Ten days to the start of autumn, and it feels like it. I'm almost too cold to sleep. But the cold gets my mind whirring—it's another problem to be solved, another distraction. I start listing all the things I need to survive: permanent shelter, blankets, a coat. Back in Takvik, I convinced a twelve-year-old boy to trade me his boots for most of my coins. I'm not sure I got the better deal. These are coming apart in five different places. I add new boots to my list.

At least, in my bag, I still have three jars of honey. Maybe I can go back to that tavern and see if they'll pay me like the baker in Takvik did.

Men's voices wake me at dawn.

I sit up with a jerk.

Danger danger danger

For a moment, I don't know where I am. These aren't my trees, my rocks, my dirt, the ones I grew to know at the top of the mountain. The morning light has turned all the shadows backward. My heart shoots into my throat and I scramble to my feet. Sling my rucksack over my shoulder. Raise my knife.

"I think I saw her over here," a man says, his voice muffled through layers of leaves.

Danger

I could climb this tree. No, branches too tall. Hide in the hollow? No, I have to run. The creek? Too shallow.

"Shh," another man says, close.

Fight back.

Clementine's knife glints silver and sunrise pink.

Branches break. I spin. Something bounds forward, toward me, and for a second, my heart is going so fast, I think it's going to split my ribs. But then I exhale, laugh, because it's not a man. It's not even a cat. It's a doe, staring at me through big, unblinking eyes.

I lower my knife.

I saw her *over here*.

Not me. The doe.

"Go," I whisper, and she does, vaulting over a low tree branch and disappearing into the tangle.

My foot lands on a twig. *Crack*. I hear a *whiz* like a swooping bird, and then something wet and fleshy.

It takes a moment for the pain to register.

When I feel it, my legs give out. I hit the ground hard, and then there's a new pain—blood welling on my tongue where I bit it.

There's an arrow in the dirt a few feet from me. It sliced clean through my filthy trousers and took a pen-sized gouge out of the side of my calf. I should be grateful it didn't hit bone. The blood is coming fast—not flowing but *spurting,* turning my hand cherry red when I touch it and the ground beneath me wet. Black flutters across the edges of my vision.

"You get her?" one of the men says.

Footsteps.

I try to haul myself away with my elbows. A rock scrapes my stomach. I'm trying so hard not to make a sound, but the pain is building, and I want to scream.

A man's voice reels off a list of expletives, then says: "Come over here."

More footsteps.

I look back over my shoulder and see two men—hardly more than boys—standing beside the tree where I slept. For a second, I think one of them is Wes. No. Not Wes. Their faces are familiar, though. We went to Keswick-Fleming together. Felix Davenport, whom I hated, and August Something-Or-Other, who mostly left me alone. They've gotten taller and started growing beards, but I still recognize them. Felix's muscles look too big for his straining skin. August is as pale as a birch tree and just as spindly.

I try to say something clever but cough instead.

"Is that Thea Fowler?" August says, horrified. "Did you shoot her?"

"Did *you* shoot her?" Felix counters. "Does Price know she's here?"

"Wes or the commodore?"

"Wes, obviously. Weren't they always tripping over each other at Keswick?"

"How should I know?" August asks.

Felix's smile turns cruel. "Rumors."

"Shut up," August mutters. To me, he says, "Do you, um, need—"

Felix punches August's arm. "Her mother is a *pirate*. The whole family's always been crazy, you remember that. This is probably a trap."

They scan the forest like Clementine might leap from a high branch at any moment.

"We can't just leave her here," August says.

Through gritted teeth, I say, "Yes, you can."

My leg sings with pain.

"The commodore'll be livid if he figures out we shot a girl," August tells Felix.

Maybe it's because the commodore is opposed to violence, but I'm fairly sure that's not it. I think back to Clementine telling me we had to leave Valonia: *What would women be but a reproductive commodity?*

I start crawling again. The pain is nauseating. Every heartbeat seems to send more blood shooting out of me.

"Let's just go," Felix says. "We can still get that deer."

"Okay," August says. "Fine."

I keep crawling through the dirt long after their footsteps are gone. I'm sure I've left a trail of blood and flattened grass through the woods, but I can't just stay there where they know to find me. *My bag.* When did I lose it? My honey. Those few coins I had left. The panic tries to rise, but I'm already at full panic. Everything is so badly wrong that I've reached transcendence.

I roll onto my back and stare at the canopy of trees. They sway, shiver. I wish I'd stabbed Felix with Clementine's knife. Or maybe I wish that I wish I'd done that.

The bulbous clouds overhead look like fat sharks.

At Keswick-Fleming, our science classroom looked out on a reef where sea lions basked. Sometimes, white sharks would arrive in frenzies, and as we watched, the science teacher would tell us how the female sharks were longer and heavier than their male counterparts. During one frenzy, our faces all pressed to the window glass, Felix put one hand on either side of my shoulders and breathed in my ear. No one noticed because the sharks were too gruesome and exciting, and I held perfectly still because I was afraid of the way Felix would sneer if I shoved him away.

Is this why Felix is willing to leave me for dead? Because I wasn't interested in him when we were fourteen? Or, almost worse, maybe he doesn't remember. Maybe this is the evil worth fearing: not that the world is out to get me, but that the world doesn't care.

. . .

The next time I hear branches breaking, I'm ready. It's close to sunset. I think I must've drifted off at some point, but I'm not asleep now.

I hold up my knife as a shadow appears between the branches. If Felix comes back, I'm going to kill him. I will. I really will.

"Thea?" Wes says.

My knife wavers. "What are you doing here?" That's what I mean to say, anyway. But my tongue is swollen in my mouth. The words spin, the trees spin, everything spins.

"August told me you were hurt," Wes says.

"He shot me." I guess I should be grateful guns and ammunition got rarer after the eruption. Clementine has a few—as I know all too well—but I guess Providence didn't get so lucky. If you can call having guns lucky.

Wes kneels in the dirt beside me. I can tell he's working hard to keep his expression neutral. "Okay, so that's a lot of blood."

Wes was always scared of blood. Not me. We did science dissections together, and I was the one to hold the scalpel while he maintained a queasy vigil. "Scared?" I say.

"I don't blame you, but you're going to make it through this."

Now I'm mad. I wasn't saying *I* was scared. But the words are dancing out of reach and I can't figure out how to correct him.

"I'm going to take you back home, okay?" he says.

That, finally, is enough to remind my limbs how to move. I thrash out of the way, scrambling back through the dirt and away from him. It leaves me feeling like I just ran down the mountain. "No," I say.

"Thea, I really think you need to clean this."

"No!"

He stands up, eyebrows bunching. His pants are covered in dirt. On his wrist, that same leather cord I noticed last time, fraying at the end. He looks so out of his depth. Why wouldn't he be? I'm a *crazy* person. I can't take his help. I never should've accepted his book of matches. I never should've come back. I should've stayed in Takvik, or better yet, just kept walking, gone until I reached a place where no one knew the name Fowler and when men shot me in the woods, nobody came to rescue me.

"Let me help you!" Wes says, almost angry in his confusion.

"No," I say again.

"You could die."

I stare back at him. "Then let me."

He dips his head, chin to chest. Finally, finally, he turns to the woods and disappears.

I collapse on the dirt. I didn't realize how much my arms had started shaking.

Wes doesn't get it, and I wouldn't expect him to. But I can't be Libera. I can't, I can't, I can't.

Once he's gone, I see what I've done with a terrible clarity. I really am going to die. I'm choosing figurative strength over actual, literal life.

I think it's what Clementine would've told me to do.

I *know* it's what Clementine would've told me to do.

CHAPTER THIRTEEN

THEN

SIXTEEN YEARS OLD

TANAGER ROCK

Every time *Asterope* docked at Tanager Rock, I went to visit Bauer. Clementine didn't know where I went when I disappeared. I think she liked the idea that I was getting more independent, leaving the ship in a hurry and keeping my mouth shut when the crew tried to pry. What did she think I was doing? Something virile, maybe, like wandering through the woods and musing at the nature of things. Or fishing. Or getting drunk on rum.

If she'd known it was about a boy, she never would've allowed it.

That made them all the more precious, the days I spent with Bauer in hidden corners of Tanager Rock. Whenever I visited, he produced another whale rib. The visits began to add up, building to something bigger as surely as the loose pieces of bone became a skeleton. I thought of the year not in weeks and seasons but in moments of Bauer.

We walked to the northern tip of Tanager Rock to see all the trees burst to blooming: a meadow of cypress, of creeping sage and broomrape blossoms. Bauer tucked a flower behind my ear while I watched his leather shoes twist the foliage underfoot, tearing stamen from stem. We stood on the beach and skipped stones over the waves. When I saw the tide pools, I didn't think of Wes.

Then, on a day hot enough to make the tanagers go quiet, Bauer tied a blindfold around my eyes. It was an old but pleasantly soapy-smelling rag from the inn, and his touch was soft.

"Why are you so dramatic?" I asked. My voice was high, laughing.

He put one hand on my shoulder, then the other. "To preserve the element of surprise, of course."

"For all I know, you're about to walk me off a cliff."

I didn't just hear his voice; I felt it, rustling wisps of my hair against my cheek. "I wouldn't walk you off a cliff."

"Is that a fact?" I said, teasing.

"Oh, you know you trust me."

When he took off the blindfold, we stood in front of a silty lagoon. Turquoise water; muddy earth.

He dared me to climb up the craggy rocks surrounding the lagoon and jump. He even did it first to show me it wasn't that hard. To show me he wasn't afraid of baring his muscled body to the sun. He leaped and howled with delight, cratering the water with a spray of mist.

I didn't want to jump. My intuition said: *This is a bad idea. What's the point of jumping? If you climb up there, you'll be exposed.*

But Bauer smiled and said: "I thought you were supposed to be a pirate."

I climbed.

I was shivery in the clingy fabric of my camisole and underwear. Annoyed at myself for being embarrassed. Distracted.

My foot landed wrong. On a bit of moss-slick stone. I went down on the rocks, spinning, felt my head bash something sharp enough to make everything go black, black, black. The water was so deep in my sinuses, in my eyes and in my pores, that I thought I'd become part of it.

Clementine never would've slipped on a rock.

My eyes flicked open and I thought I saw her, there under the surface. Shape rippling, a goddess waiting to greet me in the afterlife.

When I was yanked from the water unceremoniously, it wasn't Clementine above me. It was Bauer. Bauer's arms, Bauer's breath.

He cradled me. I was quivering and helpless, like the inside of an oyster scooped from its shell. I was a damsel, distressed, rescued by someone tall and strong. He shushed me gently.

"Put me down," I whispered.

He pushed wet hair from my face. "Good thing I was here," he said. His lips pressed against my forehead. "You could've died if I hadn't been around."

And then, a voice, a voice I tried to keep separate from thoughts of Bauer—

"Thea?" Clementine said.

I *had* seen her. I saw her through the water from the bottom of the lagoon.

The fact that Bauer and Clementine were suddenly in the same place knocked my world out of balance. I'd worked so hard to keep them away from each other—not just them, but the versions of myself I was around them.

"What are you doing?" Clementine asked. Her voice was cold.

Bauer pulled me tight to his chest, but I pushed him away. Drew myself out of his arms to stand on unsteady feet.

"With me," Clementine said, jerking her head to the path. "Unless you want us to sail without you." She said the last part over her shoulder, already walking away.

I grabbed my bundled clothing.

"Thea." Bauer seized my hand.

I turned back. Looked at him. Bauer, with his gaze soft, his lips pinched with worry. I mouthed *sorry* before I could think better of it. What, exactly, was I sorry for? I let go of his hand and ran.

"I didn't know we were leaving Tanager Rock so soon," I said when I caught up to Clementine.

Nothing.

"Did Livia tell you where I went?" I asked. "She saw me back at the inn. Leaving to—I just wanted to swim. It's so hot."

Nothing.

I hugged my dry clothes tighter to my wet stomach. "Clementine?"

Clementine stopped, there on the overgrown path, and gave me a look like—

Like the way she used to look at Mount Telamon, waiting for it to erupt. Like she knew something the rest of us didn't, and we were all going to regret not listening to her.

"You know," she said, "you won't always have a boy to come rescue you."

She turned, and she didn't look over her shoulder to see if I followed. She didn't watch for me.

I glanced back to see if Bauer had caught up. To see if he watched for me.

He didn't; the forest was still.

"I wasn't going to drown!" I shouted. I wasn't sure which one of them I was shouting at. "I don't need someone to save me!"

In response: the drip of perspiring leaves; mud drying under a too-hot sun; the echo of my voice, unanswered. So I coughed at the water still lodged in my lungs, and I followed Clementine.

All the while, something vicious picked at the edge of my shame. Something like rage.

I didn't want to be rescued. Then. Ever. I would survive on my own two feet.

You could've died if I hadn't been around.

Watch me.

CHAPTER FOURTEEN

NOW

SEVENTEEN YEARS OLD

GALATEAN MOUNTAINS, EAST OF PROVIDENCE

I wake in a puddle of sweat. The shapes of the trees overhead turn themselves into whales—long stripes of stomach and shivering strands of baleen. The sun is just beginning to set, and I should be getting colder, but instead, I feel hot.

A palm-sized tin, a little dented, sits beside my elbow. I pick it up. Frown. Then I notice the rest gathered at my feet: a bucket of water and a folded rag. I look around the woods, but I don't see Wes anywhere.

"I said I didn't want help," I mutter, but I open the tin anyway. It smells sterile. Some sort of salve. Probably expensive. What would Clementine do?

I don't want to let a boy save me. The goddess Thea, the strongest of the heroines, would never. Then again, I could die of infection. Did I mean it when I told Wes to let me die?

The salve stares back at me.

Well, if I die, I lose all future chances to prove my strength.

Even if this is the weak choice, at least I'll be alive to make the strong choices in the future.

I peel the shredded remnants of my trousers from my leg. The skin is wet and raw. I bite down hard as I dab the wet rag against my bloody calf. Sticky salve clings to my fingers. It hurts worse than the arrow did.

As I hold the salve to the light, inspecting what I just stuck in my wound, Wes appears among the trees. I jump. He's a lot quieter than Felix and August were.

"Hey," he says.

I tense. As his eyes land on the salve, I wait for him to say something like, *I knew you'd come around,* or, *You're welcome,* or, *You trust me.* Instead, he sits where he stood, back against the trunk of a tree, far enough away that he couldn't touch me if he tried.

"What is this?" I ask.

"It should keep that from getting infected," Wes says.

"Again, what is it?"

He winces. "I'm not exactly sure. It's from Valonia. We haven't figured out how to re-create it."

"I thought you were supposed to be brilliant."

"Okay, ow."

"How long have I been lying here?" I ask.

"All day."

"It feels like a week."

"I think you'd be dead if it had been a week."

"And you're sure I'm *not* dead?" I say.

The corner of his mouth twists up. It's such a familiar smile. I look away, back to the blood-streaked rag beside me.

Part of me thinks I should crawl into another tree hollow until I can make my way to my next settlement, but I've already chosen weakness once today. And I'm so tired.

"Do you know if my grandparents are alive?" I ask.

Wes pauses at the unexpected question. "I think they died during the eruption," he says. "If they're alive, they're not in Providence. I'm sorry."

I shake my head and quickly regret it—more nausea. "It's fine. I figured as much."

Maybe there was a part of me, once, that imagined coming back here and living with them. Asking Grandpa Morgan what he'd had in mind with those last words he spoke to Clementine: *At least let us take Thea.*

"Just because we all lost people," Wes says, "doesn't mean it's fine."

I don't look at him. Don't want to talk about it. "How did you find me?" I ask.

"August told me you were out here," Wes says. "He may have undersold the degree of your injury."

"Are you and August, you know, together?"

Wes's eyebrows lift. "Why would you say that?"

"Because Felix was being an ass."

"Felix is always an ass," Wes says. "And, for the record, no. But we were. About a year ago."

I watch him scrub a hand through his hair, mussing it. When

we were all at Keswick-Fleming together, I don't know that I ever saw Wes and August speak to each other. Wes was busy spending time with me, and August was friends with the contingent of toadball players. The game involved hitting toads. I thought Wes and I hated toadball players.

Even in the privacy of our shoreline, Wes and I didn't talk about our crushes—maybe because we were too young, or maybe because Clementine convinced me that admitting feelings of affection for someone was akin to admitting defeat. But on this one hot day, when we were fourteen, Wes and I were out looking for mussels lining the walls of a cove. I got so sunburned my skin started to peel. For hours, Wes had been acting fidgety. I kept poking him until finally, finally, he said, "Can you just stop talking about Declan?"

Declan was my father's research assistant. He was ten years my senior and would die in three months' time, in the same earthquake that killed my father.

I'd been affronted. Declan had just given me a vial full of iridescent fish scales. And maybe I'd liked the attention.

"What," I'd said, teasing, "are you *jealous*?"

"Of you or Declan?" Wes had said.

"Why would you be jealous of me?" I asked.

He crossed his arms. "Maybe you're not the only one with a stupid crush on Declan."

"I don't have a stupid crush on Declan! I thought you had a stupid crush on Annie Davenport."

"A year ago!" he said. "Maybe I have a stupid crush on a

different girl now. I have stupid crushes on a lot of people."
And then he'd started to cry.

I sat down and wrapped my arms around him as he talked about the cruel things his father had said about two of his officers, both men, he'd found together. About how much he'd wanted to tell me sooner, but that he'd been afraid I wouldn't get it.

I remember resting my chin on top of his head and saying, "I love you, idiot."

And I remember meaning it in all the ways.

It was one of those things we'd never said to each other as friends; he wasn't sure which way I meant it, and once it was out of my mouth, I got scared and wished I could take it back. Three weeks later, we had that almost-kiss, that night on the skiff staring at the stars. And then Clementine was whisking me away, and anything that might have been was gone.

I'm glad Wes got the chance to find someone. I hope August was a better choice than Bauer.

"What happened?" I ask.

"He hated Clipper," Wes says.

"Your dog? No one hates Clipper."

He almost smiles. "Nothing happened, really. We just didn't have anything to talk about. And any questions I may have had about his morals were reaffirmed by the fact he was willing to shoot and abandon you in the woods."

"In Clementine's book," I say, "that probably makes someone a *better* prospect."

Wes's expression grows serious. I shouldn't have said that. Why bring Clementine into this?

"My father sailed yesterday, by the way," he says. "To go find her."

I swallow. The rush of blood in my ears is so loud, it seems impossible Wes can't hear it too. "Well, good luck, Commodore Price."

"If you want to come back to our house to get some food and sleep in a real bed, he won't be there. I don't know if that makes you more or less willing, but there you go."

"I'm fine, thanks."

"You're making it really hard to help you," Wes says.

"Good," I say. "Why do you feel like you need to help me?"

"Do I need a reason? Shouldn't the default be that I *want* to help people, and I need a reason not to?"

I eye him skeptically. "Why were you in the apothecary when I first saw you?"

"I work there."

"Aren't you a little young?"

He makes a humorless sound—a laugh that's not a laugh. "A little young, a lot incompetent. When we first got here, I agreed to be the doctor's apprentice. Doctor, singular, because exactly one doctor made it here from Valonia. He died of a fever that wouldn't break two years ago."

"So you're the doctor. For all of Providence. Even though you're scared of blood."

"I'm not scared of blood anymore."

I squint at him.

He wraps his arms around his knees. "I'm no more excited that I'm Providence's *only* doctor than anyone else." With a shake of his head, he adds, "I still can't say that with a straight face. I sound like such an asshole. *Doctor*."

"The town trusts you with something as big as all that?"

"It's me or no one, unfortunately," he says.

"What do you get out of it?" I ask. "Nothing?"

"Out of *helping* people? Being kind to people? Everything."

I don't say anything to that. His earnestness rubs me the wrong way.

Wes frowns. "I'm not saying you have to trust me. But you have to trust *someone*."

"Why?" I ask. "We're all too selfish in the end. Even the people you think you can—the people who really . . ." I break his gaze. Stare at a spot of setting sun between trees until my eyes water from the brightness.

His voice is soft. "It's worth the risk."

"What is? Because as far as I can see, it's never worth it."

"I guess that no matter how many times people hurt me, or break my trust, I just . . . I think of a time it didn't go that way. Of a person who showed it could go differently."

I'm thinking of August when I say, "How?"

"In my experience," he says, "you say a lot of things and cry and make a fool of yourself, and they say, 'I love you, idiot.'"

I look up.

His back is pressed to the tree. In this light, his skin seems to glow, all studded with freckles like stars.

My stomach twists.

This is how I pictured Wes. All those years away from home, this is how I pictured him. With his hair pushed out of his eyes and his face smudged with dirt and a leaf clinging to his shoulder. Cold nights alone, while *Asterope* rocked, while the wind lashed her sides—when I shut my eyes, this was how I pictured Wes.

And that terrifies me. It terrifies me that I feel myself softening to him. I've accepted his help once, twice, so why not forever? Will he just be the next person in a long line of people I mold myself to please?

He shuts his eyes, just for a breath, long shadows from his eyelashes feathering his sharp cheeks. I watch him. Hold my breath. "You're safe here, Thea," he says. "We're allowed to be friends. Clementine's not watching over your shoulder."

I can't breathe.

It's so, so like something Bauer said to me. *Your mother's not watching over your shoulder anymore.*

"Has it occurred to you that I don't want to be your friend?" I say. My voice is getting tight, and my eyes are starting to burn. The only thing worse than feeling a feeling right now would be letting it happen in front of Wes.

"After all these years," he says, "are you really still trying to prove yourself to her?"

"Eat shit, Price."

"You shouldn't have to," he says quietly. "Prove yourself."

I look away from him.

Are you really still trying to prove yourself to her?

When have I ever been doing anything else?

He stands up slowly. I hear him brush the dirt from his pants. "Coming to my house is too much. Got it. But if it's okay with you, can I come back tomorrow?"

"Do whatever you want," I mutter.

"What do *you* want?" he asks.

After a long, long silence, I say, "I'd take the quarter inch of my calf back."

I know it's not the answer Wes wanted, but the truth is, I'm too afraid of asking for half the things I want. I'm afraid to tell myself that better is possible. This is my life now.

Asking for more always backfires.

At sunrise, Wes isn't back. My leg feels a little better. I feel better. For a minute, with dew and young sun on my skin, I am radiantly happy. I'm going to see Wes today; go to his house today; maybe eat some honey today. What a day to be alive.

When the fear arrives, I fall all the farther for my moment of hope.

The forest shivers. Bends in on me. The dew is too cold; the sun too revealing. I gather the salve and haul myself up by the trunk of a tree.

It's strange, that the hope shows up before the fear. It makes me angry. I can visualize the fear now: like a big wall locking me out of half of my brain.

After an hour of stumbling through the forest, I can't find my rucksack. Honey, coins, flint, all hard won, all easily lost.

Maybe I *should* go see Wes. As soon as I think it, the *what-ifs* start spiraling away from me.

What if he's only being kind to me because he sees me as a thing to possess?

What if he wants to lock me up and force-feed me hysteria tinctures?

What if he turns me over to Clementine?

I press my back to an unfamiliar tree in an unfamiliar clearing and let the bark scrape my shirt up as I sink to the ground.

What if he's simply kind, and I don't deserve it?

To imagine a new future for yourself is to tempt fate. I made that mistake once before.

When I fell for Bauer, I didn't just fall for a boy. I fell for the version of myself I imagined with him. And when I imagine letting myself get close to Wes, it's not just Wes I picture. It's the Thea who never became a pirate. It's the Thea who studies science and roams the tide pools and is not afraid to love and be loved.

But it's just an illusion. Right? It's not possible. Wes can't give me any of that. No one can.

I apply more salve. I hear branches breaking as someone or something clomps around in the distance. I say nothing.

Eight days to the start of autumn. Livia and Clementine will be sailing to the cove by now. I wonder if Clementine has a third ship and a third captain yet.

I curl in the crook of the roots and stare at my hands: the parched, flaking skin; the black dirt haloing my nails.

I'm thinking about Bauer in my periphery. It's not that I

want to. It's that he lives there, just out of sight, always watching me, whether or not I turn to watch him.

Leo Bauer.

What's his middle name?

The question jolts me, because surely I know it. I knew it at one point, didn't I?

Sometimes, there's part of me that wonders if I shouldn't have just stayed with him. He's probably earned a paycheck by now. He probably sleeps under a roof instead of a rock. He probably has friends who laugh at his jokes. What would I have become if I hadn't left? Would I have gotten quieter, ever quieter, until my voice box shriveled to nothing? Or maybe I would have found a way to silence the thing in my head saying *No, this is wrong, he is wrong.* Maybe I would've eventually silenced that voice like he silenced me.

To stay would've been painful, but this is painful too, so sometimes, when I'm especially hungry or cold, I wonder if I chose the wrong pain.

Maxwell.

His middle name is Maxwell.

I press my hands to the dirt, absorb its cold, and I breathe.

Sometimes, I wonder if I chose the wrong pain. And then I forget his middle name, if only for a minute. It's such a good fucking minute. To know that he does not mean everything. To know that my future is not him. To know that today, it might only be his middle name for a minute, but someday, it might be his face, his words, his laugh.

I push myself up.

It's a new day, and I can take whatever pain it brings me.

I start walking.

PART THREE

THE MYTH OF LIBERA

THEN AND NOW AND THEN

Then and now and then, the gods married.

The king of the gods and the lord of the sea, hotheaded Saleus, was the first to pick his bride. "I choose Thea," Saleus said. With crafty Thea at his side, he would never be outsmarted.

"Surely not, my king," Thea said. "My sister, Libera, is the fairest of the goddesses. She will bear you many sons."

Saleus considered. "Very well," he said. "Libera shall be my queen."

The next god to choose a bride was Saleus's brother Telamon, the storm-bringer. Jealous Telamon was angry Saleus had claimed Libera, and he did not trust crafty Thea. But of all the goddesses left, Thea was surely the fairest. "I shall take Thea," Telamon said.

"Oh, no," Thea said. "You would prefer my other sister."

"You have no other sister," Telamon said.

"I do. Tonight, I will introduce you, in Saleus's temple."

That night, Telamon arrived at Saleus's temple to find the loveliest creature he had ever seen. She stood very still near the altar.

"Yes!" Telamon said. "I shall take this goddess as my wife."

But when he rushed to meet her, he realized Thea's trick—she was a statue, painted in cosmetics and wrapped in women's clothes. Telamon bellowed in anger.

Curious Libera saw the whole thing. She had known, after all, that Thea had no other sister. When Telamon spotted her, his jealousy consumed him.

"Thea promised me her sister!" he raged. "So her sister I shall have!"

Telamon had his way with Libera, producing four children: the gods of the wind, each of whom would buffet Saleus's seas.

When Telamon was done, he cursed Libera. He had been humiliated by a statue, so a statue Libera would become. With a wave of his hand, her skin turned to white marble. She was frozen like that in her husband's temple.

When Saleus returned, he was furious at Libera's transgression. He chose not to unfreeze her, preferring to admire her silent, horrified beauty. With the goddess of mothers and children turned to stone, there was no one to protect mortal mothers. Childbirth would be painful forevermore; for Thea's betrayal of her sister and Libera's betrayal of her husband, all women would be punished.

Chapter Fifteen

Now

Seventeen Years Old

Providence

It takes me two hours to find my way out of the forest, but I do it. I end up far north of Providence, so I have to trek back to the cliffs to the place where I once hammered on the Prices' door.

The last time I was here, it was night, and my vision was fuzzy with anger. In the light, I see it clearly: The villa is more dilapidated than I first realized. In the fountain, the statue of Saleus is missing his fingers and stained with soot. In a garden around the side of the house, a few undersized pumpkins grow from vines.

A blur of white shoots past me. I whirl, primed for danger. But it's a dog. He comes up to my knees, but his cloud of fur makes him look bigger than he is. Mud stains his paws.

I catch hold of his collar, where a metal tag reads: *Clipper.*

"Hey, boy," I say. "Remember me?"

Clipper slept at the foot of Wes's bed every night, no matter how many ways Commodore Price tried to lock him out. He showed up at Keswick-Fleming at least once a week, his big nose bumping the window of our classroom and prompting the teacher to either sigh or tell Wes to bring him in, depending on the teacher. Wes and I made up a secret code and named it after the dog—Clippish, we called it—where we added an *ip* before every vowel sound and talked fast enough to infuriate Commodore Price. My father helped us fashion Clipper a soft leather collar with a name tag on it. With the leftover scraps of leather, Wes and I tied bracelets around each other's wrists, and I felt so buoyed by this marker of friendship, this *us* I was a part of, that I thought I might float away. It sounds silly now, sentimental and sappy, the way anything good does when you're older and jaded, but when Wes quadruple-knotted my bracelet so it wouldn't ever accidentally fall off, he told me, *"Bipest fripiends."*

Clipper licks the side of my face. I'm pretty sure Clipper looks at everyone with this sort of adoration, but still. Feels good.

"Thea?" Wes says.

I straighten.

He's leaning against the door frame, head tilted.

"I was hoping," I say, the words coming slowly, "that we could make a trade."

"A trade."

"I've gotten good at harvesting honey. I can sell you some in exchange for clean clothes. Maybe a blanket?"

He fights a smile. "You can just come in, you know."

"No," I say. "I want to trade."

"Fine. Bring me a jar of honey, and you can have clean clothes and water and a blanket and some bread. And maybe also a bath."

"That's too much."

"It's not," he says. "You smell awful."

"Do you have a jar?" I ask. "And more matches? I had flint, but Felix stole it." I'm not sure this is precisely true, but it makes me feel better about asking for more.

I wait as he thumps around in the kitchen for a few minutes. When he comes back, he's holding the required materials.

"Please don't die just to get some honey," Wes says.

"We'll see."

It's not my best day of honey collecting. There aren't any man-made hives down here, but I stumble on a wild one. Trying to cut off a slice of honeycomb without destroying the hive reminds me that I have no idea what I'm doing. I use up four matches and am more bee sting than I am skin. My leg throbs, so I have to use a tree branch I found as a walking stick to keep the weight off of it. But by sunset, I have an elegant chunk of honeycomb in my jar, and only then do I allow myself to trudge back to Wes's house.

"Here," I say by way of greeting.

"Finally," he says. "Now will you stop trying to get your leg infected?"

"Only because of our trade."

"Yes," he says. "Fine. Please, come in."

Inside, there's a big kitchen, dining room, living room space rolled into one. The furniture is a combination of the new—rough wooden chairs with imperfect edges—and the old—a blue velvet couch with water-stained cushions. Opposite the chimney, there are three doors, which I take to be Commodore Price's bedroom, Wes's bedroom, and a bathroom.

"Do you want tea?" he asks. "I have peppermint."

"What about my blanket?" I ask.

"I didn't forget. But want tea first?"

"Fine. Sure. Thanks."

I watch him move through the kitchen. Setting a kettle to boil. Fishing dried leaves from a jar. It reminds me of watching my father cook when our staff had the night off.

Wes pours two mugs. My hands, dirty and bloody, look out of place against the sage-green earthenware. But it smells nice, and the heat feels good.

"I'm nervous my father is going to get killed," Wes says.

"By Clementine?"

"Yes. Are you nervous for her?"

"No," I say.

He drums his fingers against the side of his mug, watching me. Thinking. Finally, he asks, "Why'd you do it? Why'd you tell him where to find her?"

Because she's a killer. Because she deserves to be caught. Because I got angry.

"I don't know," I say quietly.

"Okay," Wes says.

Eight days until the autumn equinox.

A long, long pause.

"Why didn't you tell me you were leaving Valonia?" he whispers.

I look up and find him gazing at me over the top of his mug. His dark eyes are serious and sad.

"She didn't tell me," I say. "I had no idea."

He looks away. Presses the mug against his cheek. "I'm sorry none of us believed her. When she told us about Mount Telamon."

"What difference would it have made if you believed her? You were fourteen."

"Still. I could've talked to my father, maybe. I could've—"

"You couldn't have done anything, Wes. It was too late. I wasn't even sure if I believed her. If I did, I would've fought harder to get more people to safety."

He looks up at me again. For a moment, it seems like we're both asking each other for absolution that neither of us can give, so we just stare, hollow, regretful.

"Why didn't you come here after the eruption?" he says.

"She liked being a pirate too much," I say. "Or she was still bitter no one believed her. Or . . ." I shake my head. "There was one thing she said. About repopulation. She thought there might be so few Astorians left that she and I would be married off against our wills and told to have a bunch of children."

"That," Wes says, "is a terrifying thought."

"Clementine having more children?"

"No. *Me* having children." He presses his lips together. "Being told who I'm supposed to marry."

"Ah. I forgot that seventeen-year-old boys are all meant to be terrified of marriage. Have to sow their wild oats?"

He leans back. It's just a little thing—a tiny movement—but still, I can tell he's hurt, and I wish I hadn't spoken.

"That's not what I meant," he says.

"I'm sorry," I say. He doesn't accept it, but he doesn't reject it, either. "Did you ever talk to your father about August?" I ask.

Wes takes a long sip of tea, stalling. "My father has . . . changed."

"Because he was so warm before?"

"He's even harder to talk to now. I don't know how much you heard about what happened to us when Mount Telamon erupted—"

"Not much."

Wes nods. "Well, the top twenty most likely candidates for Person-in-Charge all died. The only reason we survived was that the headmaster at Keswick-Fleming thought our class could use some 'toughening up,' so he sent us to my father for the day. We were on my father's ship learning about sails and how terrible the navy is, and then—you know. The eruption. We weren't that far from shore, but it was far enough to survive. We joined up with some of the others who managed to get on ships in time and found this place. It was the only Astorian land we could find that wasn't covered in ash."

"No one lived here?"

"Not for a few hundred years." By way of explanation, he adds, "The famine."

I wince and nod. One of many curses that caused Astoria to contract.

"Everyone started planting seeds as best as they could. Storing water. Fishing. And everyone voted for my father to be the first governor. He organized everyone, so people felt . . . grateful."

"It sounds like he saved a lot of lives."

"He did," Wes says.

"But . . . ?"

"The silver lining in a catastrophe is that you can remake things better than they were. But he's so concerned with rebuilding what we had in Valonia that he's started acting like it was perfect. And I just don't see how a bigger population and more elegant houses means we've made a better world."

"Clementine talked about that a lot," I say. "Breaking free of expectations, I guess."

"I disagree with her methods, but she's always been clever."

She is.

Eight days.

I'm not worried.

"This honey is really good," Wes says, lifting his spoon from his tea. "I might need to change the terms of our trade so you get your money's worth."

"I see what you're doing, and I'm not falling for it."

"Sleep on the couch? Or you can take my room. Or my

father's. Whatever you want, really. It's freezing outside, and you have to take care of your leg."

I need to say no, but I want to say yes. The tea is warm against my scratched throat, and I just want to curl up here forever.

"If it were just me, obviously, I'd tell you to leave," Wes says. "But Clipper missed you, and I'm so bad at saying no to him."

Clipper, as if on command, presses his nose against my hand.

"Only until my leg is healed," I say. "And I'll sleep on the couch. And get you more honey."

"Deal," Wes says.

The next morning, as I towel myself off after my first bath in over a month, I feel a sense of stillness. Goodbye, grime. Goodbye, guilt. I know you'll be back, but for right now . . .

In the kitchen, Wes is already up. There's a bowl of hot porridge on the table.

"Putting on the same clothes sort of defeats the purpose of the bath," Wes says.

"I feel fantastic," I say.

"And covered in dried blood."

"I look heroic and dashing."

"And like you just did battle with a mountain lion."

I consider that. "That's fine by me," I say.

He points to the porridge. "Eat fast. I want to show you something."

We take the winding path down to town. On the way, Wes points out a stretch of geometric fields in varying stages of deadness.

"And . . . those are?"

"Beans, flax, potatoes, buckwheat. We're trying everything to see what works on this soil."

I inspect the yellowish stalks, the barren fields. "And is it? Working?"

"Nothing seems to grow here," he says. "And before you say anything, yes, I do see the irony." He gestures around us—the trees, the tumbling grass, the wildflowers. "Everything grows here. Except the things we're trying to grow."

We keep walking.

When we get to the apothecary, the jewel-toned bottles wink at me from the window. I flinch, feeling guilty.

Wes pushes open the door and motions me through the shop to a room in the back. He holds aside a sheet of canvas to let me go first.

"What is this?" I ask.

"Welcome," he says, lighting an oil lamp, "to the University of Providence."

It's just one big room. The walls are covered in maps: the familiar contours of the Astorian Islands and a gestural length of continent. I also see charts of elements, diagrams of the solar system, and botanical illustrations of plants and animals. A workbench stretches across one wall. On it sit a microscope, an open book, and a pile of haphazardly assembled fish bones.

When I see the skeleton, Bauer pokes at my periphery; I tell him to fuck off.

"What are you working on?" I ask.

"Anything," Wes says. "Everything. That's my problem. Before Evan—he was the doctor here—died, I spent most of my time researching. He would tell me that someone needed a pain reliever, or that he had to set a broken femur, and could I figure out how he was supposed to do that? We lost so much when the volcano blew. I have stress dreams about all those books buried under ash. Really makes you wish you'd listened to that lecture on antiseptics."

"That's what the salve you gave me was, right? To fight infection?"

"Yes, and we have exactly six of those tins left, so I really wouldn't mind figuring out how to make more."

"When we were kids," I say, "you wanted to be a marine biologist, not a doctor."

"They're not hiring many marine biologists these days, unfortunately." He almost smiles. "But I don't mind this. It's useful. I haven't slept in three years, but at least I'm doing something."

Doing something.

My heart is full with possibility and potential. I listened during science class. I sat at my father's feet as he told me about all the expeditions he went on, all the things he saw. *Asterope's Revenge* was full of books, a solace away from Clementine's expectations.

"Are you hiring?" I ask, trying to make my voice light, as if I don't care.

Wes turns to look at me. Very seriously, he says, "Can you provide three professional references?"

I stare back at him.

"I thought you'd never ask," he says.

By my third day at Wes's "University of Providence," he hasn't yet left me alone. It's not that he doesn't trust me—he trusts me too much, probably—but that he doesn't trust the town. I think he's worried Felix will come back with his arrows.

Back in the main room, I hear a bell jingle. Wes gets to his feet, glancing at me. I stay put.

He never tells me to stay back here, hidden. But I always wonder, when he looks at me like that, what he's thinking. If he's scared of me, or embarrassed.

Once he's out of sight, I tiptoe after him. I pull the canvas flap to the side just far enough to see into the main room of the apothecary.

A girl in a plain, whey-colored dress stands at the entrance. Di. Her fingers are knotted nervously.

"Has the midwife from Fairshore arrived yet?" Di asks by way of greeting.

"Not that I know of," Wes says. "Why?"

"Then we should start getting supplies ready. In case."

I wonder if the *in case* they're talking about is Hanna's

pregnancy. I have exactly zero desire to be helpful to Bauer's sister, so I keep hiding behind my canvas sheet.

"Supplies?" Wes says, his voice pitching higher. "I thought we had another month."

"My mother doesn't think so."

"Great. Fantastic. And I have exactly how long to become a learned scholar of midwifery?"

"Calm down," Di says. "You know, my mother *has* had children before." She gestures to herself. "All the same. She wants you to check on Hanna."

Wes exhales slowly, and I can't take my eyes off him. He looks so *adult*—it shouldn't be allowed. We're the same age, yet here he is, busying himself with medicine and childbirth. The way he holds himself too—his shoulders back, his chin high. He's glued himself together with sheer force of will, and a lonely, young part of me aches for my old friend, for the boy who would do anything for anyone.

He comes back to the research room in a few strides, and I have to leap out of the way so he doesn't know I was spying.

When he pulls aside the canvas, he gives me a curious look.

"You're okay alone here for a while?" Wes asks me.

"Fine," I say. "If Felix shows up, I have a knife."

"Perfect," Wes says, looking like he doesn't think this is actually all that perfect.

They leave, and I go back to my reading. I've spent the day poring over a trio of unrelated textbooks, pinging from one to the next whenever I start twitching. I feel the same constant thrum of anxiety I felt in the forest, gripped by the need to do *something*. At least this brand of *something* might be useful.

The first book is on genetics, written by one of Grandpa Morgan's students. There are probably a few interesting kernels of information on genetic disease, but so far, all I've found is impenetrable writing and some seriously troubling justifications for male aggression. If Wes ever gets anyone else involved in the university, I'm removing this one from the curriculum.

There's another one on marine biology. Wes has clearly gone through it a hundred times already.

The last is actually about medicine. With anatomical diagrams and references to experimental surgeries, it *should* be the most useful of the bunch. Unfortunately, it's severely water-damaged, so I spend about an hour per page trying to decode, then rewrite, the information. It's slow, tedious going, hence the textbook hopping.

When Wes gets back, I push the genetics text toward him and say, "This book is stupid."

He looks tired. The bags are heavy around his eyes. But he still comes to look at the stupid book in question. "Why?"

"It says women are naturally more emotional, and that this is a proven fact because their tears have a different salinity."

"That sounds improbable," Wes says.

"I know! Let's burn it."

He winces. "Can we just flag it as unlikely? I'm scared to burn anything that might save someone's life."

"Fine," I say, grabbing a pen. "But it *is* stupid." I pause with my pen above the page. I wonder if Clementine believes things like this. She certainly didn't like emotional women, but I don't know if she blamed science or culture. "You know, Clementine told me strength comes from not being governed by your feelings. For women, anyway."

"Just for women?" Wes asks.

I don't answer that.

In the past few days, the more time I spend with Wes, the more concerned I get about his relationship with his father. When we were kids, Commodore Price wanted Wes to join the navy. But now that Wes has become the de facto keeper of knowledge, Commodore Price seems to ask an outrageous amount of him. Research everything. Know everything. Preserve everything. Wes keeps a list of topics he's been asked to research or dig up books on, along with the names of who requested the information. Some of the topics with *Com. Price* next to them: blasting powder, mining, combat medicine, steam power, religion and superstition, breeding livestock, soil acidity, textile crops, cesspools. While the pirates stop the settlements from trading goods, they also stop the settlements from trading information. But no one trusts anyone, and more books turn to campfire fuel or ocean rubble every day.

So I keep reading.

I don't know if any of the books Wes gives me will end up being important. All of them, none of them. But I know that it feels good to try. To wake up my brain and demand something of it. *Oh,* it feels good to feel alive again. When I fall asleep, sometimes my mind is so busy picking at the threads of things I read that day that it forgets to be nervous, angry, afraid.

Four days to the autumn equinox, not that I'm thinking about it.

My leg is doing, if I'm honest, fine. I still keep a bandage wrapped around it, but it's healing well. I keep trying to make sense of water-damaged science texts and notebooks. I bathe regularly and go to bed with a stomach full of thin, hot soup and bread; there's not a lot, but there's enough.

It's too good. It can't hold. The better things get, the more convinced I am that they will come crashing down spectacularly. The more I let myself hope that this is a real future, a real life, the farther I'll fall.

I don't know if I can survive a fall from this height.

CHAPTER SIXTEEN

THEN

SIXTEEN YEARS OLD

TANAGER ROCK

The eighth time I met Bauer, I finally asked him about the whale ribs.

Asterope had docked at Tanager Rock in advance of a wall of dark clouds. The rain hadn't yet started falling when Bauer handed me the eighth whale rib. So far, he'd shown me one every time we'd met. There wasn't room for a whale rib cage in the inn, so we were assembling the pieces out back. We were by the shed where his parents kept spare plates and tankards and bed frames. Between the shed and the twining trees, I couldn't see the ocean, couldn't see *Asterope,* couldn't see Clementine. Just me and Bauer in the world.

"You don't really find one bit of bone every time I'm away," I said. "So where's the rest of the skeleton? It must be washed up somewhere secluded."

"I don't know what you mean." His eyes were bright, catching shards of the quickly fading light. "Whenever I find one, it's a sign that you'll be back to see me soon."

"But I'd like to see the full skeleton," I said. "I was reading a book on whale anatomy, and it said that the bones of a whale flipper aren't so different from a human hand. Can you believe that some scholars are still arguing that a whale might be a fish instead of a mammal? Or . . . were." I wasn't up to date on what, if anything, scholars were arguing these days.

His blithe smile never wavered. "I wish I could help, but it's like I said. The bones appear like magic."

I let out an irritated breath through my nose. I knew he liked games, and I did too, but I wished that everything wasn't a game with us. He didn't need to always surprise me, always make things magical. Sometimes it felt like he'd read too many stories about charming heroes. And it worked, at first. His charm. But charm got tiring. I would've preferred honesty.

"Well, maybe your magic can send me a flipper next time instead of another stupid rib."

Bauer turned from me, but not before I saw my words land and stamp hurt across his face.

I stood up. Took his hand.

"I'm sorry," I said. "I didn't mean that."

He wouldn't meet my gaze.

"Bauer," I said, tugging his hand. "You know how much I love—love the skeleton. Only you would think to do some-thing like this."

Technically, as I had been involved with exactly zero other people, I wasn't sure that *only* Bauer would think to rebuild a whale skeleton together. But it seemed like the thing to say.

And it worked. He smiled back at me. Cupped my cheeks

in his palms and kissed me. I kept my eyes open, watching the honey curls of his hair, the tanned width of his face. And then, on the ridge of his forehead, a fat raindrop. It splattered us both.

He stepped back. We both looked up. The clouds, not so long ago just a bad omen on the horizon, seemed low enough to touch.

"I love that smell," I said. "Rain smell."

"You know what I smell? Food. Let's go get dinner. We can eat in my bedroom."

I wanted to stay longer. Get my fill of rain and wet earth. But he was already walking inside, and I was starting to shiver, so I followed him.

I went behind the bar out of habit. Bauer and I had spent plenty of evenings there, talking between filling pints and collecting coins from the counter. Last time, Bauer had even let me serve a few drinks with him, so that's what I did, eager for something to keep my hands busy. I took a man's order and passed him his lager.

A year ago, I wouldn't have believed it. That I would be at home behind the bar at the Tanager Rock Inn. That I would know what lager was.

Bauer fell into step beside me. Brushing his hand along my arm to let me know that we were okay.

Once we'd cleared through the customers who didn't yet have drinks, Bauer turned to face me.

"What happened after you left me at the lagoon?" he asked. "You never told me."

I left him? That's not how I would've phrased it. I supposed he was right, but at the time, it had felt more like he was abandoning me.

"Nothing," I said. And it was almost true. Clementine never mentioned Bauer to me. She never told me I was being stupid or that I should find better things to do with my time than swimming with boys on Tanager Rock. She also never asked who he was. How I felt about him. If I kissed him or loved him or was sometimes frightened of him and of my own desire. She said— nothing. When she talked to me, she talked about readying me to captain a ship. Livia had already begun sailing her own, and she was a natural. Clementine had been putting off the third ship, though. No one on her crew wanted to sail under my command. No one thought I was ready for the autumn armistice, now just two months away.

Bauer broke my gaze, sulking. "You've met my parents."

"Your parents aren't pirates."

He took my hand. "I know you love her. But you shouldn't feel this way about your own mother."

"Feel what way?"

"Afraid," he said.

I dropped his hand. "I'm not afraid of her."

"You told me she was always pushing you to steal things, break things, yell. She's a good pirate. She's heartless." He paused. "You're not."

He didn't mean it as an insult. Still felt like one. I looked out the window, at the rain coming down hard, and pressed my itchy palms to my thighs. I wanted to run outside and drink in the rain, escape, let it sweep me away.

Bauer pressed his hand against the bar so hard, I could see his knuckles turning white. "Can't you see she's manipulating you? She's made you think that you need to be this terrible, cold girl, hurting people, and—and Thea, that's not you. You're better than that."

We looked at each other. He stared at me more fiercely than I'd ever been stared at.

No one had ever told me I was better than Clementine. At anything.

He reached out to take my hand again. This time, I let him.

"There's something I didn't tell you about," Bauer said. "Because I was sure you'd say no. But . . ."

I stepped a little closer, ready to hear anything—everything.

"There's a whaling ship," he said. "They've come through a few times, and I met the captain. You know how badly I want to leave Tanager Rock."

My mouth felt dry.

"They agreed to take me," Bauer said.

"How soon?"

"When the weather clears."

Two days, then? One?

"You weren't going to tell me?" I said.

"I was always going to say goodbye," he said. "I just didn't want to spoil things too soon. But then I started thinking . . ." His teeth caught against his lower lip. "Come with me."

"What?"

"You could come with me," he said. "You know how to sail.

Maybe they'll let you join the crew. And you won't have to listen to Clementine ever again. It'll be the two of us on a big adventure. No more parents telling us how the rest of our lives are supposed to go. Just us."

My heart was beating hard and fast. From fear or excitement, I couldn't tell.

And then Bauer kissed me. Like he was hungry and like no one was watching. A cheer erupted on the other side of the bar, and I pushed away. My cheeks were burning again.

I hardly dared glance at the patrons. They were watching us.

My voice low, I said, "I can't. You know I want to. But—"

"But you won't leave your mother," Bauer said. He was already turning back to the empty glasses on the bar. "I know."

I watched him pick them up. Drop them in the sink. Water and beer splattered the edges of his filigree curls.

I shouldn't have even been thinking about it. But I was.

A different future.

He painted such a perfect picture. And whether or not he believed it, so much of me really did want to say yes. But how could I leave Clementine? My only family left? I couldn't.

So I'm not sure why I said: "Can you give me a day to think about it?"

Bauer looked up. Smiled. "Thea," he said, "I'd give you the whole world."

The night wore on and the storm got fiercer. The rain came down vengeful, splitting trees and flooding the path. No one could get back to their ships. Bauer and his parents laid sleeping rolls and blankets across the floor to make extra beds once the rooms filled up. I almost wished Bauer would invite me to take Hanna's bed in their old room, but his parents were watching, and he didn't offer. I supposed we'd be spending plenty of time together if we went on his whaling ship.

I found Livia. She'd taken a corner of floor and welcomed me into her nest of blankets.

That night, I lay awake to the sound of rain and drunken snores. I stared at the ceiling. The blurry shadows of lantern light reflected against wet windows.

Could I really run away from Clementine? With a boy?

But no. It was always about more than just a boy. It was about a future.

In two days, I'd turn seventeen. Seventeen was old enough for my own life, wasn't it?

My future had always been Clementine's to devise. For most of my childhood, I was supposed to be a scientist; then, suddenly, I was supposed to be a pirate captain. And until Bauer, I never knew there was a way out.

But when I stood behind the bar, I was someone else. Sailing away with Bauer, I'd be someone else. Not a pirate. A different girl. With a different future.

Chapter Seventeen

Now

Seventeen years old

Providence

When Wes and I walk through town, I try to not be noticed while not revealing that I don't want to be noticed. I recognize about a quarter of Providence—August, Felix, and a few other Keswick-Fleming boys; Di and her mother; an elderly couple who I think knew my grandparents. But even those who don't know me shoot me odd looks when I pass.

Wes and I are coming back from a trip to the sprawling collection of herbs on the other side of the river. It was supposed to be a small garden, apparently, but the mint got viciously out of control, and now it's less a garden and more a field. Mint is the one thing they've planted that's grown. Wes told me that while most of Providence stays alive by fishing, a few families have taken charge of farming, and they've asked him to come up with an insecticide to protect their turnips from aphids. One of the books we looked at suggested using mercury, but another book pointed out that mercury poisoning is distinctly unpleasant, so Wes is now looking into using mint.

The air smells like hearth smoke and the mint bunched in our hands. Though it's noon, the fog hasn't burned off yet—it never really seems to—and the forest is just a hazy idea. Wes and I match steps, our legs moving together on the chipped stone path.

"My qualms are threefold," I say.

"Your qualms?" Wes says.

"One, won't mint just invite its own host of mint-eating insects? Two, why are we so sure mint will get rid of aphids? What are they scared of? What's mint hiding from us? And three, we're spending an awful lot of time trying to save a few turnips, and honestly, I'd just as soon leave the turnips to the aphids. Can't we grow something else?"

"Like?"

"I don't know. Strawberries."

"Ah, yes, the nutrient-dense and famously insect-resistant strawberry."

"Who put these families in charge of farming, anyway?" I ask. "I don't know that I trust anyone who loves turnips so much."

"My father put them in charge. There was a big meeting. People offered their skills. Look, most of us were from the city. We're figuring it out as we go. One family had an extensive backyard garden not far from Keswick-Fleming. Another man was a rancher on one of the western islands."

"The western islands!" I say. "I thought all they grew were wine grapes."

"And turnips, apparently," Wes says.

A flash of purple fabric flies in front of me. I jerk backward, narrowly avoiding colliding with a girl as she sprints across the path and seizes Wes's arm. Di.

"The baby's coming," she says. Her hair is sticking to her face with sweat.

Wes's smile drops away. "You told your mother?"

"She's already there."

Wes and Di do an about-face and start heading back to the edge of town. I'm left standing blankly in their wake. I know exactly zero things about babies, much less what to do when they're showing up for the first time. But I also don't want to keep standing here helplessly. And as Wes has the key to the apothecary, I can't go back there.

I run after them before they can turn the corner out of sight.

I follow them all the way to a tiny marble cottage with ivy climbing up the walls. It would be quaint if there weren't screams coming from inside. Di goes in first, and Wes stops and turns to look at me.

"You don't have to come in," he says. "It's a birth."

"I gathered that," I say. "Is it Hanna Bau—Hanna?"

Wes nods. "And the baby's coming early. And we haven't exactly had a lot of . . . successful births in Providence."

"Why not?"

"Because it's complicated and we're all idiots!" Wes whispers. "As you're about to find out."

"Oh." I feel ill.

"Are you coming or not?" he asks.

I hear Hanna shriek in pain. For a minute, a sick, angry part of me thinks, *Good!* What should I care if a Bauer is in pain? I owe Hanna nothing. Less than nothing.

My chest is tight.

I owe Hanna nothing, except my nothing would never get back to Bauer. He would never think, *Ah, yes, my sister had no one to hold her hand during the delivery of her child. That Thea Fowler really showed me.* He wouldn't care. He probably wouldn't ever ask for stories about the birth at all.

Not helping Hanna doesn't punish Bauer. It just punishes Hanna. Is that enough? Do I *want* to punish Hanna?

When men get angry at each other, they fight. But when women get angry at men, we can't fight back, can we? We have corsets and pretty shoes and malnourished figures to worry about, all these tricks to keep us from fighting physically, and when we fight verbally, even the most eloquent rebuke can be dismissed with that singularly wretched word: *irrational.* So women must turn their anger on each other because there's no one else to hold accountable. No one else who might listen. No one else who might hear a woman's roar and think it powerful. And when a woman—out of charity, exhaustion, or some hard-won insight—realizes the futility of tearing down the women around her, she has only one place to funnel the seething, smoking, acrid pool of rage that has been building since she was a child: back on herself.

Not today, Leo Bauer. I see your tricks and today, I'm too smart for them.

I follow Wes through the door.

Inside, Di's mother stands at attention by a box of ointments, towels, and bottles. Di hovers at her side. And then, of course, Hanna herself, lying red-faced and sweaty on a bed at the room's center. Not that Wes, with his blank, greenish expression, doesn't look totally capable of handling this on his own, but I'm relieved there are women here, at least one of whom has given birth before.

I can't stop staring at Hanna. Her hair is the color of shortbread. Unlike Bauer, her eyebrows and lashes are almost transparent, but mostly, they look exactly the same. She's so pretty. I wait for a panic that never comes. The memories tickle but don't pull me anywhere.

"Good," Di's mother says. "Price, I need alcohol."

"Is now really the time?" Wes asks.

"I imagine it's to sterilize things," I say helpfully.

Her gaze snaps to me. "Here," she says, gesturing me over. "I'm going to instruct, and you're going to listen."

If she's concerned about what Clementine's daughter is doing in her town, she doesn't show it. I set to work rubbing down a pair of scissors as Hanna makes uncomfortable noises. At one point, Di says, "You're doing great," to which Hanna snaps, "How would you know? Every baby born here dies."

Everyone shares an uneasy look over the top of Hanna's head. I'm starting to understand the crowd in the room now. Wes might not be an expert, but I suppose he's better than nothing if—*complications* arise.

Hanna drops her head back. "Pirate girl," she says. "Murder me. I'm begging you."

Wes's head snaps toward me and he narrows his eyes.

"Probably talking to someone else," I say.

I'm saved from explaining when Hanna screams, the loudest scream yet. Her hand flies out, and I don't know what I'm doing, but I take it, my sweaty palm against hers. She squeezes so hard I think my bones are going to break, but I squeeze back anyway. *I'm here. I'm here. I'm here.*

The myth of Libera says this is supposed to be awful, childbirth, and maybe that's why we don't work harder to fix it. The myth of Libera says that women are cruel to each other and women deserve what they get, that Thea betrayed her sister and look how much pain it caused.

But I'm a Thea too, and I'm not going anywhere.

The birth doesn't make me want to wax poetic. Maybe this was supposed to be a turning point for me, wherein I saw the power of the female body and the bonds of motherhood and daughterhood that link us all.

But I still thought it was pretty disgusting.

Once it's over, the baby daughter safely nestled in her mother's arms, Hanna seems to see all of us anew, like she'd forgotten we were there. Her eyes snag on me, and I wait for her to say something, either about Bauer or that day we met in Providence. She doesn't. She just smiles faintly and nods. There's a lot packed into that nod, I think, and I'm too tired to inspect all the pieces.

Wes and I were, thankfully, largely unnecessary. Wes is

making himself look busy by sorting through the tincture bottles.

"How are you feeling?" Di's mother asks.

"Fine," Hanna says. "Tired."

I realize for the first time that Hanna's less attractive husband has not yet made an appearance. "Where's Gideon?" I ask.

Her face goes very blank—a mask. "On a voyage," she says. "He'll be back."

There's a tension in the room that I don't understand. I glance at Wes, but he just shakes his head once.

"What are you going to name her?" Wes asks.

"Nothing with a meaning," I say. "It's bad luck."

"You don't like being named after a myth?" Hanna asks. "I always wished I had a story behind my name."

"At least you're not named after your father," Wes tells me.

"I'd make an excellent Phin," I say.

"It's too confusing," he says. "And you run the risk of being called *Junior*."

"I've already made up my mind." Hanna smiles down at the baby as if it's beautiful and not very red and squashed. "Melody."

"Oh, bad choice," I say. "She's going to sing like nails on chalk."

Wes elbows me. "You can't just tell someone they chose a bad name for their baby."

"What?" I say. "She did."

Hanna ignores me, which might be for the best.

I think she's going to be a good mother. Why? I don't know.

Something inside me just says, *Yes, see, see how she loves that girl already.* I busy myself wiping blood from the floor. But when I look up, I watch the way Hanna looks at her daughter. She smiles like there's light inside her; like she swallowed a sunrise. Like this little girl has made her phosphorescent, and as long as they're together, they'll never stop shining.

I bend my head to the floor and scrub.

There's a knot in the base of my throat, but I don't let myself make a sound.

By the time we leave, the sun has set. We never got the chance to make that mint insecticide. I'm actually not sure where all the mint we collected went. I think we left it on the path. But this, I'm realizing, is how most of Wes's days go: a long race to put out the highest burning fire even though the only firefighting equipment he owns is a bucket of dirt.

I'm surprised to find that I don't feel afraid, walking through Providence at night. I know the way back to Wes's house. I'm not checking around corners to see if I'll get shot.

Don't get complacent, Clementine's voice in my head whispers, but I'm too tired to pay much attention to her.

"You know Hanna," Wes says.

I consider lying. "I guess."

"How?"

I consider lying harder. "Her brother," I say finally, "is my least favorite person. Including Felix."

"Oh," Wes says. "Do you want to tell me why?"

"Not particularly." I pause. "What was that thing about her husband? You gave me a look."

"Oh. Ah. You're not going to like this."

"Why?"

"My guess is that Hanna's husband left, and she was afraid we'd say something. There were rules in Valonia about what rights a single woman had—"

"Please," I say. "You think Clementine didn't make sure I knew all of them?"

"Right," Wes says. "Well, I suppose she's just scared."

If there was a time when I would've been pleased to know that Hanna, like me, has dealt with stupid men, that time is over. "Well," I say, "Gideon seemed tedious anyway."

What hope is there in Providence, in this little village by the sea, of a woman and her child surviving on their own? I don't know. But I hope more than there would've been in Valonia. It's so small here, and everyone knows everyone's name, and everyone seems to have a job to do. And I hope people help Hanna and her baby, just like they did today. She's up against the odds; up against holdover prejudice from the world we left behind. But she's still doing it. She's still here. The thought gives me hope for my own future—if Hanna can survive, so can I; if I can survive, so can Hanna.

As we walk, I touch the knife at my waist. I haven't taken it off since coming to Providence, except to bathe, at which point I've kept it on the side of the tub. It's becoming less of a weapon and more of a safety blanket.

What if Bauer had shown up? He still might. Dock here to

visit Hanna. What then? I decided there was no use in hurting Hanna, but what about hurting Bauer? No women need be used as collateral damage. Except, of course, me, because if I killed Bauer, I'd probably get force-fed hysteria tinctures for the rest of my life. Or executed. Still. Would it make me feel better? Clementine was a big advocate of revenge. She'd say yes, of course.

But I don't know. I just don't know.

It's the last day of summer. Somewhere on the sea, Commodore Price could have just glimpsed *Asterope's Revenge*. Somewhere, Clementine could have just raised a gun and pulled the trigger.

I sit with my feet curled under me on one end of the couch, Wes on the other. We're drinking more peppermint tea. I made it this time, and I didn't need to ask him where he kept his tea or how he took it. We both take it with honey.

We sit in companionable silence for a few minutes, sipping slowly.

"You don't have to tell me if you don't want to," Wes says finally. "But why did you leave Clementine?"

I look up at him, surprised. "Did your father tell you anything?"

Wes frowns. "Why would he tell me . . . ?"

"Because," I say, "he was there when I ran."

Chapter Eighteen

THEN

Sixteen years old

Tanager Rock

The morning after Bauer told me about the whaling ship, I slipped out of the Tanager Rock Inn at dawn, leaving Livia sleeping on the floor.

I found Bauer behind the inn, feeding goats again.

"Bedhead," he said, ruffling my hair.

I ducked away from him and crouched with the goats instead.

"Will you miss them?" I asked, staring into a little one's rectangular pupils.

Bauer tossed a bundle of weeds at them. "No. They're just goats."

"Will you miss me?"

"Last I checked, you weren't a goat."

I looked up at him. He leaned against the railing of the pen. From below, the light made his hair look like it was on fire.

"So you're not coming with me?" he asked.

"I'm . . . thinking about it. You're sure the captain would be okay with it?"

Bauer shrugged. "They take wives all the time. Voyages can be long."

My skin prickled uncomfortably. "I'm not your wife."

"I'm just making a point. I thought it was men who were supposed to get scared of the W-word. Anyway, we'll drop you off at a settlement if you don't want to sail with us, and then I'll come back for you once I've made some money. It'll work fine. The captain said he's leaving at dawn tomorrow."

"I guess . . ." I looked down at my hands. "I guess I'm just worried—"

"Come on, Thea," Bauer said, already turning away. "You know you trust me."

I did.

Didn't I?

At Keswick-Fleming, we'd had a marine biology lab lined with eerie, greenish tanks. The science teacher kept clams and crawdads and rare kelps for us to study. But the most unnerving tank was the octopus. She'd watch us while the teacher lectured. She'd watch me as I gathered my books. I'd stare at her, and she'd stare back with uncanny intelligence. Stick her tentacles against the glass like she was asking me to take her with me.

And then, one morning, we got to school, and she was gone. She'd escaped. The only evidence was the tank lid, pushed aside; a trail of water leading to the sink. We all huddled around it. Stared down the pipe. It seemed entirely too small for an octopus. But the science teacher told us, chagrined, that an octopus could squeeze its boneless body down to the size of the hole between my pinched thumb and forefinger.

I spent a long time wondering about that octopus. Whether she made it to the ocean. What it felt like, squeezed inside that metal pipe. How she knew to take the sink to the drains to the open sea outside.

That morning, I felt like I finally understood the octopus. Two futures lay diverging before me: be Clementine's captain; run away with Bauer. I had to choose soon, and I felt squeezed.

I picked my way back to the harbor. *Squeeze, squeeze, squeeze* went the walls of the pipe around me. I wanted to get out. But out of where? To where?

When I got back to *Asterope's Revenge,* the crew was gathered on the rain-slick deck. Clementine's voice boomed.

I climbed aboard, my stomach doing little twists.

Clementine spun. Her eyes latched on to mine. Her smile was crooked, and for a moment, I thought she was going to tell me she was tired of me disappearing with Bauer, and that I'd never go back to see him again.

"The storm held me up," I said. "Sorry I didn't make it back last night."

"Guess who I caught prowling the harbor," Clementine said.

My stomach gave another unhappy lurch. "Who?"

Then Clementine stepped aside. I saw a man tied to a chair on the bow. His hair was dappled black and gray; his eyes were squinted against the sun. He was dressed like someone dignified, in a smart jacket and leather shoes, but tied down in that chair, not much dignity was left.

Clementine smiled. All malice.

"You must remember," she said, "the esteemed Commodore Wesley Price."

Chapter Nineteen

Now

Seventeen years old

Providence

The day of the autumn equinox.

I fold the blanket neatly over the back of the couch and straighten my pillow. Make myself a cup of peppermint tea, drizzling spoon after spoonful of honey across the thin surface. The hot cup burns my hands, but I keep them hugged around it anyway.

The cove is a week's sail from here, so it's not like I'll hear about her victory for days yet.

I go outside to feel the cold ocean air. It's autumn, all right. Down the cliffs, the waves are the color of steel and flint. From my vantage point, I can see all of Providence: the slow-moving river and the little shops; the beach where I hauled myself to shore; a ruined lighthouse beyond it all. Clipper presses his nose into my calf, whining softly.

Wes finds me out there.

"What are you looking at?" he says.

"The sea," I say. "She's angry today."

"They won't be here for a few more days."

"I wasn't watching for them."

"Okay," Wes says. "How's your leg doing?"

"Fine. I saw Felix yesterday, by the way."

"Really? When?"

"When you went to check on Hanna," I say.

"What did he say?" Wes asks.

"Nothing. He looked like he saw a ghost."

"I'm sure you got no pleasure out of that."

"None," I say.

A week in Providence, and people are starting to realize I exist. I keep waiting for something awful to happen, but it keeps not happening. It's a tenuous peace. Do I let myself dream that I could stay here? Spend my days recovering lost science and my nights sipping peppermint tea?

I want this peace to last. I just don't know if I deserve it.

The ship arrives five days after the equinox, so at first, I think it can't be the commodore. Saleus Cove is a week's sail from here.

But he's a better sailor than I gave him credit for.

I'm sitting outside when it happens. It's cold but sunny, and I find a bit of only slightly damp grass along the side of the apothecary. My back presses to the stone. I face the ocean with a book against my knees, the wind riffling the pages. Wes is with Hanna again, as he has been all morning, making sure she and the baby are healthy.

My book is about stars. I know the constellations already—

have known them since I was a child—but there's something old and grounding about tracing the silhouettes of Thea's spear and Libera's bassinet. They guide us home across whatever dangers the sea sends us. I imagine stargazers finding the shapes long before me; others dragging their index fingers through the skies long after I am dead. It makes me feel like I'm part of something permanent.

And then, from the harbor, shouts.

I frown.

I can't quite make out the words. I put a blade of grass in the book to mark my page and stand, swaying slightly. My calf still hurts when I put weight on it. I press a hand to the side of the apothecary and squint to the harbor.

Commodore Price's ship.

My heart leaps to my throat.

Calm down. He's back because he failed.

I tuck the book under my arm and start to run. Between the apothecary and the harbor, there's a narrow dirt path a quarter-mile long. Grass swishes against my ankles.

Clementine is fine. I'm not scared.

A thin crowd gathers around Commodore Price's ship. As the sailors dock, they're met with frantic waves from children and happy cries from wives. I don't see Commodore Price.

Clementine is invincible.

And then, striding across the deck, with his broad shoulders, with his nose and cheeks so like Wes's, Commodore Price. Behind him, two sailors. Between them, a woman with her hands cuffed together and a gag in her mouth.

"Clementine?" I whisper.

She has scratches across her face and a black eye. Her hair is wild; her eyes, even wilder. She looks rabid, feral, furious.

Commodore Price's chest is puffed out. He's gloating.

I take a step back. My body collides with the trunk of a tree. I'm fifty feet from the harbor, but Clementine would see me if she thought to look this way. I know she'd see the truth written on every part of me. *Coward. Traitor.*

My breath is fluttery, air in my mouth but not my lungs, dizzy-making.

I thought telling Commodore Price how to find Clementine would make me feel strong, but I don't feel strong at all. I feel like a villain, or a child, or a fool—all of the above. Did I ever imagine he'd actually outsmart her? Of course not. But he did. He won. He was the powerful to her powerless.

If Clementine is not invincible, then nothing I know is true.

The trees wrap cold and familiar around me. Like they knew I'd be back. Like they knew I'd never make it in Providence.

I cling to the edge of the forest as the sun arcs overhead and sinks behind the horizon. As Commodore Price and his men take Clementine through town, I stay in the shadows like the coward I am. Pragmatic Thea says: *This is wise. If Providence sees how distraught you are by Clementine's capture, they'll never trust you.* Angry Thea says: *You're just afraid to see the look on Clementine's face when she realizes what you've done. What you are.*

The town comes out to watch her, like it's a parade. Commodore Price is so proud of himself. Clementine screams through her gag. From the safety of the trees, I watch Wes emerge from the apothecary. He glances left and right, eyebrows drawn together. Worries the leather cord on his wrist.

When Clementine passes him, she lurches forward like a dog about to bite. Wes leaps back. Commodore Price shouts something, and the sailors guiding her tug harder.

I search the pit of my stomach for the anger that got me here. *Get angry, Thea!* I reach deep down for the feeling that gripped me when I thought: *Oh, Clementine. I will show you what my fire can do.*

All that's left is embers, smothered by cold, clammy fear.

They bring Clementine to the ruined lighthouse on the far cliffs. I expected some sort of jail, but maybe Providence doesn't have one. In the three-hundred-person settlement, how often do they consider arresting someone?

I follow them to the lighthouse, keeping myself hidden between trees. Pine overwhelms my senses: the crinkly smell of it, the sap on my fingers, the dry needles crackling underfoot. The heel of my hand is skinned and raw; I must've fallen. I don't remember.

Up close, the lighthouse looks even more desolate. The walls are crumbling, but I can make out evidence of where it might've once looked grand. The sea spray has stained it, bleached it, bitten it, but here it stands.

As the sailors shove Clementine through the door, she twists her head to glower at them. For a moment, I swear her eyes land on me. But then she's gone, and I'm sure it was just my fear getting the best of me. Commodore Price goes in after her.

Three sailors stand guard around the lighthouse. One has a gun; the other two have crossbows.

I stay among the trees as minutes drain by, waiting for Commodore Price to reappear. My feet fall asleep, so I sit, back against a tree. I think I hear a voice at one point—Clementine's venomous shout—and I sink deeper into the ground.

A squirrel darts past me. Close enough that I could touch it. So close, it's like it's forgotten I'm a human and not just another forest thing.

I wish I were.

I wish I could turn into a tree. A silent, harmonious *thing*. No love, no fear, no mother, no nothing. When I speak, bad things happen. When I don't speak, bad things happen. It would be better if I had no mouth at all.

The pine needles dig through the fabric of my pants. In my throat, the air is too dry to breathe.

Clementine shouts again, and that's all it takes to unravel me. I'm as brittle as the pine needles. Silent, hot, angry tears start coming down my face. I press my palm against my mouth, the scraped palm, and it *burns* but I bite down anyway.

A tiny sob escapes me, and one of the sailors' heads jerks up.

Come on. Come *on,* Thea.

Be quiet.

Be quiet.

Be *quiet.*

It's the only thing you've ever been any fucking good at.

My eyes blur. With tears, with pain. I don't know. I couldn't say how much time passes. But when Commodore Price finally comes back out, he's smiling.

"Did she tell you anything useful?" one of the sailors says.

"Not yet," Commodore Price replies. "Even a pirate bitch is loyal to other pirates, apparently."

More loyal than I am.

"How long are you going to wait for her to talk?" the sailor asks.

"I'm not a patient man. We already sent word to Fairshore and Silver Creek."

Sent word? My arm slips, and the tree behind me creaks. Commodore Price looks up.

"You hear that?" he says.

He and the sailor squint at the trees, but only for a minute.

"Ah, well," Commodore Price says. "I'll see you in the morning."

As he leaves, he whistles.

He *whistles*.

How long do I sit there? Long enough to see the guards ebb in and out of conversation. Why is everyone so cavalier? I want them to show, if not sympathy for Clementine, then at least grim determination. I want them to care.

I'm begging someone other than me to care.

"You have a cousin in Fairshore, don't you?" one of the sailors asks.

"Haven't seen him in months now. You know how Fairshore

is. Hoarding their good luck—no need to trade with the rest of us. Even family."

"Maybe this'll change the tide."

"Has to. If we don't start trading with the other settlements soon . . ."

I strain for any sound from inside the lighthouse. Clementine's voice. A cough. Anything. But it's quiet. Is she afraid? Of course not. What's her plan? Will the rest of the crew show up, or did Commodore Price stop them somehow?

My head is throbbing with the beat of guilt. I'm guilty, and I'm afraid, and I'm alone.

No. This is stupid.

I'm going to talk to Commodore Price myself. I was the one who told him how to find Clementine. He'll talk to me.

I'm wobbly getting back to my feet. When I try to wipe my eyes, I smear dirt in them. I'm sure I look like a mess, but I feel even worse.

By the time I reach the Prices' house, the sun has set. Clipper starts barking before I can knock. When Wes opens the door, I spot my blanket folded neatly over the edge of the couch. My mug, still half-full of tea.

Commodore Price stokes a fire in the hearth. When he sees me, he stands quickly. His mouth does a complicated series of movements—a proud smile, like the sight of me reminds him of his triumph over Clementine, then a cautious frown, then a neat, stoic line.

"Thea," Wes says, "where have you been?"

"I saw you caught Clementine," I tell Commodore Price. My voice wobbles. I hate it.

"I did," Commodore Price says, still watching, still trying to read me. "The settlements are safer today than they've ever been."

"What's going to happen to her?" I ask.

"Why?"

"Are you going to kill her?"

He sizes me up. *Loyal, disloyal?* "You're the one who told me how to find her."

"Next week," Wes says. "They're going to hang her next week."

I make a noise. Clipper whimpers, pressing his nose into the back of my leg. Wes is looking at me with great concern; it makes me want to burst into flames. Clementine is going to hang. Next week. My fault. I know I turned Clementine in. I know I was mad. But maybe there's part of me that still wants—needs—her to be proud of me. I need to show her that I swam and fought and survived.

Can't I be mad at her while simultaneously wanting her not to die? Can't she be less than a hero and more than a villain?

I thought I could survive without her, but now, abruptly, I'm absolutely positive I can't. What am I without my volatile, decisive, stoic, exacting, irascible, audacious, crazy pirate mother? No one. Nothing.

"You can't," I say. "Can't you do something else? You have to do something else."

"We can't risk her escaping," Commodore Price says. His voice is businesslike now, like my horror has strengthened his resolve. "If you knew how many lives she's responsible for ending in the settlements—"

I do know. That's the worst part. I know that when we stole food, people starved. When we stole ships, people were vulnerable. When we sailed across the horizon, people were afraid to trust each other.

But I still don't want her to *die*.

"Why a week from now?" I say. I feel like an animal trapped in a cage, flailing, looking for any opening. "Why not a month? Or a year? Maybe she can tell you more about the other pirates. If I helped—if I talked to her—maybe she could be useful. To Providence."

"She hangs in a week," Commodore Price responds. I'm starting to make him impatient.

Impatient. Not worried. Important distinction.

He doesn't think I pose any threat to his plans. He's annoyed by me, but he doesn't bother wondering if I'll break Clementine free. Why would I? I'm just a girl, hysterical.

"Why a week?" I ask again.

There's a long pause.

"The spectacle of violence," Wes says.

"Wes," Commodore Price says sharply.

"What?"

"They're waiting for other settlements to arrive," Wes says. "Thea, I'm sorry."

The sailors at the lighthouse said the same thing—that Fairshore and Silver Creek were coming to Providence, and that it would change things. That it had to.

Of course. Clementine and the other pirates have ruined every chance the settlements have had at establishing trade. They've all been hurt by her. They all hate her. She'll die, and more people will live. The settlements will find peace, prosperity. They will learn to trust. They will celebrate the spilling of her blood, the snapping of her neck in a noose.

The spectacle of violence.

Oh.

"Please," I say to Commodore Price. "Please, she can be useful. You don't have to kill her. Please. Please, I'm such a—*please.*"

His eyes, uncomfortable, fix on my ear. "Perhaps you should go."

I grab his sleeve. "*No—*"

"Wes, get her off of me."

I feel hands on my shoulders and heat in my face. Clementine can't die. If I had shot Commodore Price when she told me to, if I hadn't run away with Bauer, if I hadn't told Price how to find her—

"Come on," Wes says.

Commodore Price straightens his jacket and turns back to his fire, face as smooth as though I never spoke at all. Wes guides me outside.

"Please," I say one last time, but then the door closes, and with it, I feel the finality of Clementine's death, sentenced.

It's dark outside. The wind whips off the ocean in cold ropes of salt. The lights of town flicker—soft yellow candle flames against the cocoon of endless forest. It smells like falling leaves and freshly turned soil.

What does the beauty of a world mean if neither of my parents can see it?

"We can talk to my father again," Wes says. "Maybe we can still work something out. Ask for mercy, or—"

"Your father won't show her *mercy*," I say. People like Clementine and Commodore Price aren't merciful. They know how little good comes of mercy.

"Then what?" Wes asks. "What are we going to do?"

"*We* aren't doing anything."

A pause. "Thea," Wes says, too softly, too gently. "Don't try to break her out. You could get hurt. The guards could get hurt, and they didn't have anything to do with this."

I already know that.

I don't care.

"What about you, then?" Wes says. "You really want to go sail around the world with Clementine? What about saving all those books? What about the university?"

The future I let myself hope for. I never should've been so naive. Now it all seems childish. *The university*. I didn't deserve any of it.

"Be selfish!" Wes says. "You deserve *more*. Give yourself the chance to live the way—"

"Shut up, Price." And then, because I want him to hurt,

because I want him to leave me alone, I say, "I should've killed your father when I had the chance."

He flinches. I'm not who he remembers. Good.

I don't say anything that might redeem myself. I don't tell him anything that could prop open the door. I don't deserve sympathy—I don't want it.

I don't deserve love. I don't want it.

He turns away from me. Hunches his shoulders, one hand clasped around his wrist, still tugging that stupid leather cord. Still holding on to a friendship that's gone and a version of me who's dead.

"What is it you want, Thea?" he says. "To be like Clementine? To spend the rest of your life as a pirate? *That's* what makes you happy?"

"Don't pretend you know who Clementine is. Don't pretend you know who *I* am. Clementine is a survivor. She takes care of herself. *I* take care of myself." For all my fights with Clementine, that's always what she's wanted for me. Not for me to become a pirate. Not for me to become a killer.

She wanted me to be a survivor.

Wes's hand falls from his wrist.

I push past him. Keep going, keep moving, don't look back. A week. A week to figure out how to save her, even if it means throwing everything else away. I have to.

When I plunge back into the forest, I realize Wes isn't following me. I lean against the nearest tree. Give myself just a second to breathe.

Through the spindly arms of treetops, I can see stars. The spray of constellations. I trace the tip of Thea's spear rising over the horizon.

I've never believed in gods and I've never had anyone to pray to, but right now, I wish I believed.

My mother named me after you. Help me. Help me.

In the stories, the goddess Thea says that all of man's weakness comes from two places: love and fear. From love and fear come every other emotion. When a hero comes to Thea for guidance, she presses her thumbs to his temples and takes away his love and fear. She takes away his weakness.

I press my thumbs to my temples. I imagine what it would feel like to rid myself of love and to rid myself of fear.

'What is it you want, Thea? Wes asked me.

This is what I want: I want to run a scalpel through my skull, temple to temple, and free myself of love and fear.

I don't know which of the two—love or fear—is telling me I can't let Clementine die. I love her. I fear her. I want to love myself. And I am afraid of who I am without her.

If the goddess Thea were here to take my love and fear, I'd turn away from Clementine and never look back. But she's not. Love and fear fill me. Maybe they make me weak; fine. This will be my last act of weakness. I'll save Clementine, and in so doing, I will ruin the future I've started to build here. Ruin any forgiveness Wes has started to give me. I will do this one, final, weak thing, and then I'll have nothing left to hold me back. Then, for the rest of my life, Clementine and I can be strong.

Like equals.

CHAPTER TWENTY

THEN

SIXTEEN YEARS OLD

TANAGER ROCK

Clementine had tied Commodore Price to the end of *Asterope's Revenge*. He was silhouetted by sea, fringed in old stubble, and bound in ropes he didn't struggle against. A gash ran across his arm. The blood was hardened and brown.

Across the deck, the crew spread in clumps. Some of them looked entertained—smiling at the prospect of watching Clementine mete out vengeance—but it was impossible to ignore the whispers, not quite caught behind cupped hands.

She's going too far.

She have to play with her food before she eats it?

This is mental.

Clementine put a heavy hand on my shoulder and steered me toward the bow, forcing me to face Commodore Price. She had a spatter of blood along her collarbone. I pictured her flashing her knife, making that slash on Price's forearm.

He looked me up and down. "I remember you," he said.

Was that supposed to make me like him more? I spent half

my time playing on the shore in front of his house; should I feel grateful he deigned to recognize me?

"Don't talk to her," Clementine snapped. "Why are you here?"

His eyes flicked toward the ship beside Clementine's. Livia's ship. The one we stole from his harbor. "I want to talk."

"About?"

"The settlements can't trade," Price said. "Not when you pick off every ship in our waters. If we all die, so will you."

"Thanks for your concern," Clementine says, "but I think we'll manage."

The corners of Price's mouth twisted. "You always were a bitch, you know that?"

"And you always were a bastard," she said. "I heard you were elected governor. Congratulations. Tell me, are women allowed to vote? Or is repopulation the *only* thing you let them do?"

"My settlement is a good place," Commodore Price said. "It's a safe place."

"For whom?" Clementine said.

"Says the woman who grew up gilded," Price shot back. "Straight from your parents' house to Phin's. I remember being in classes with him at the university, you know." To me, he added, "Not the brightest student, but Clementine Morgan never would've married someone smarter than her."

I felt a surge of something—anger or fear or discomfort—but Clementine's face never changed. The only hint I got that she might be bothered by Price's words was the subtle tightening in pressure of her fingers on my shoulder.

"Leave my daughter out of this, Price," Clementine said.

Her voice was as chill, as even, as stoic as anyone's voice has ever been.

Commodore Price didn't look impressed. "If you stop acting hysterical, the two of us can handle this like adults."

The two captains looked at each other. I was trying not to shake.

"You'll make an excellent bloodstain on *Asterope*'s deck," Clementine said. She raised her gun and pressed it to his throat. His smile caved. Something awful happened in his eyes—this bright, dizzying flash of emotion—and I realized I was watching a man say goodbye to his life.

"Clementine," I whispered. "I don't—"

She snapped her attention to me. Narrowed her eyes.

I swallowed. "His crew will come after us if we kill him."

"Listen to the girl," Price said, pleading.

I tried to ignore him. "Please. He's trying to get inside your head."

"On the contrary," Clementine said, "I feel utterly like myself."

She was going to kill him. And there was nothing I could do to stop her. I wasn't even sure if I should stop her.

But I still didn't want to watch.

I had come to accept that Clementine wanted to see men die. That was just the way of things. My mother killed people, and it didn't make her feel bad. But where was the line? Killing a stranger meant nothing; killing an old friend meant nothing. What about killing a member of her crew? A daughter?

I shut my eyes and tried to steady my breathing.

No shot came.

When I opened my eyes again, Clementine was staring at me. Slowly, she lowered the gun. Commodore Price exhaled softly.

Clementine walked toward me. The whole crew had gone silent.

"What are you doing?" she said.

"Nothing."

"You don't think he deserves to die?"

"I didn't say that."

"Well, that's a relief," she said. "Because I thought you wanted to captain a ship in my fleet. Isn't that right? I thought you wanted to prove that you deserve a chance."

I pressed my lips together.

"I've tried to teach you that you can't expect the world to be kind and fair," Clementine said. "People will never stop trying to steal from you, and they'll never stop trying to hurt you. Do you understand?"

"Of course I understand," I said. "I'm not—"

"Then shoot him."

Silence.

"What?" I said.

She extended the gun to me. "Shoot him. I won't always

be around to protect you. If something happens to me, you're facing the world alone. You want to be a captain? Prove that you're strong enough. Shoot him."

I stared at the gun in my hand. I didn't remember taking it, but there it was, heavy and cold.

"I already know how to use it," I whispered. "I could shoot him if I needed to."

"I'm telling you that you need to."

I felt the eyes of all the crew on my back, Clementine's burning most of all. And then Price, his gaze steady on mine.

"Please," he said quietly. "My son."

"Be quiet!" Clementine snapped.

The mechanics were simple enough. A two-hand grip, because my hands were small and the recoil was fierce. I was meant to stand with my feet shoulder-width apart, knees slightly bent.

I was good with the mechanics. I'd shot plenty of rounds off the side of *Asterope's Revenge*.

But shooting at air wasn't enough for Clementine.

Nothing was ever enough.

I don't know how much time passed before Livia stepped forward. I hadn't even seen her coming down the winding path from the inn. How long had she been watching? "Just let her go," she said. "She's a child."

"Sixteen is not a child," Clementine said.

My eyes started to sting. Commodore Price, at the bow, hadn't shed a tear. His chin was still high and brave. Maybe I would've been able to shoot him if he were sneering. Or if he were sobbing. Or if I'd never seen Wes make him laugh.

Maybe I would've been able to shoot him, if, if, if. But I doubted it.

Livia shook her head. Her eyes were narrowed like she was disappointed.

The gun wavered in my hand.

"He isn't just a bad man," Clementine said. I'd waited too long already. "He's a representation of a bad system. Of hundreds and hundreds of bad men. Do you understand?"

Of course I understood. I understood that some men thought women were less than, were objects for ownership and satisfaction. I understood that Commodore Price had never treated Clementine, or me, like we were smart.

I understood that Clementine would make sure Price died whether or not I fired the bullet.

Here's what I didn't understand: why I couldn't do it.

"Kill him, Thea," Clementine said.

I shut my eyes for a moment, hoping the gun would somehow go off without my having to direct it. The trigger wiggled under my finger.

What did it mean to be strong?

What did it mean to be named Thea, after the goddess of reason?

Commodore Price could be the evilest man in the world. The trigger would still resist.

I opened my eyes. "I can't."

"Yes," Clementine said, "you can."

I shook my head. Once I said it, relief rushed over me, glorious as the first sun after a storm. I couldn't do it. Who was enough of a pirate to pull the trigger? Not me. What a fabulous, frantic sort of feeling. I was a failure! I was a disgrace!

So I lowered the gun.

"Are you my daughter," Clementine said, "or not?"

I dropped the gun. It clattered against the deck.

"I'm not going to kill him," she said. "I'm going to wait for you to do it. And you might not do it today, but you will do it."

Was I smiling? Maybe. I had nothing left to lose. Truly, this was the bottom of everything. This was ecstatic failure.

Clementine scanned the faces of the crew. Some were gaping. Oh, good. I'd embarrassed her. How hard it must've been for her. To have a daughter like me.

She grabbed my hand. Pulled me downstairs to the captain's quarters. I gazed around with detached interest. Clementine so rarely let me in the captain's quarters. Never invited me to sleep on the sofa or the other half of the massive bed. Inside, it was quiet, stuffy.

"Can't you see I'm trying to make sure you'll survive?" she said. "How do you think you'll stay alive if I'm not here to protect you?"

"Maybe I won't," I said. "Maybe someone will murder me."

This wasn't what she expected. She turned to me, eyes narrow. "I'm trying to help you."

"No, you're not," I said. "You're trying to help you."

My eyes were filling with tears and burning from the pressure of not letting them fall.

"Just tell me why you can't do it," she said. "Tell me why you can't shoot him."

I wished my father were still alive. I wished I'd had more time with him, time I could've asked him how he fell in love with Clementine and what they saw in each other. I wished I'd been allowed to know my grandparents, like family, so my grandfather could've told me about his research and my grandmother could've taught me how she navigated a man's world. I wished for a mother I called *Mother* and a future that was mine.

I wished Clementine loved me without reservation, without sense, without logic. I wished Clementine loved me the way I loved her.

"I'm sorry," I said, my voice tight.

"Don't be sorry," she said. "Just don't be . . ."

Her eyes roved across me like scalpels. *Emotional? Weak? Pathetic?*

In the end, she said nothing, which was as bad as saying everything. She turned away from me, going to the window and throwing it open. Staring at the sea like it could tell her why her genes hadn't come up with anything better than the grief-shrunken girl behind her. Her hand rested lovingly on the edge of the porthole. *Asterope's Revenge* always was a better daughter than me.

"Clementine," I said.

She didn't look back.

She ignored me as I approached the window, tears stinging my eyes. I watched her, with her black hat and her wind-whipped hair and the gun in her hand. Muscled arms and twitching jaw. That spatter of blood along her collarbone. The ferocity in her gaze, fixed on the distant horizon.

I didn't blame her for not looking at me.

Mother, I mouthed. I was too afraid to say it out loud.

Maybe she took all the strength the world allotted to Fowler women. Maybe there was none left for me.

"Clementine," I said again. I tried to make my voice sound strong. I tried to make it sound like Clementine's.

She shook her head. Sighed to the wind. "Thea," she said, "be quiet."

Chapter Twenty-one

Now

Seventeen years old

Providence

I'm worse at being in the forest than I once was. I forget to eat. I forget to sleep. What am I without Clementine? No one, nothing.

The sailors move in lazy circles around the lighthouse. I have nothing but Clementine's knife. But can I reach the sailors? Kill them quietly? Even if I wasn't at an arms disadvantage, could I *murder* three people?

It feels like fate, that it would come to this. Clementine always wanted me to be strong enough to kill, and I never was. But to save her life?

I tug at my hair, pulling from the roots. The world pulses. *This* is hysteria. *Shit. Shit!*

I sink to the ground and try to breathe.

No one. Nothing.

For three days, I watch the lighthouse.

I feel like I'm observing another species. The sailors and I are different creatures. I'm a naturalist, watching them come and go; watching them feed; watching them work. Eventually, I realize that it's not them who isn't human; it's me. I'm something wild. Single-minded.

The guards between noon and six in the evening are the best of the rotation: attentive and quiet. The midnight to six in the morning guards are the worst. They take naps, sometimes, and tend to drink and play cards when they think no one is watching. But I watch. I watch everything.

I think I'm crazy.

Fine.

On the fourth day, the strangers begin to arrive. I see their wagons coming over the hill on the other side of Providence. Their ships docking in the harbor.

The first group is fishermen, but then there are others— dozens, *families*. People bring their children. Everyone wants to see the spectacle of violence. I watch the strangers set up their colorful tents in Providence's main square. Two young girls in homespun dresses roll wooden rings through the maze of canvas awnings, squealing.

I watch for familiar faces, and I burn.

In the shadow of a headless statue, Felix tucks a loose strand of hair behind a pretty woman's ear, and she blushes. Di brings glasses of beer to a trio of sailors.

A little girl falls flat on her face. Her mouth starts bleeding. She sobs, and there's Wes, kneeling beside her.

Clementine could die, and Wes's life would go on. I could die, and Wes's life would go on. I try to take comfort in that.

The people in Providence are still people, but I'm the forest.

At any given time, only one of the guards has a key to Clementine's cell. Sneaking past them, I think, won't be hard, but getting the key will be. I figure I'll probably need to kill the guard who wears it.

I should've done it already. Gotten it over with. On the fourth night, I almost do, but I freeze up. I hold Clementine's knife in my trembling hand and watch the sailors play a card game, but I never move from my spot in the forest.

My problem is, I start wondering if this is a trap. If Clementine orchestrated all of this. She wants me to murder someone so badly that she hired all these people as actors. Or let herself get caught just to see if I have what it takes to free her. My thoughts circle and eddy and then the sun starts to come up, and better guards arrive to replace the night shift, and my opening slips away.

I'm crazy.

I'm going crazy.

I watch the strangers, but I never spot Bauer among them. Good. Once I start killing people, maybe I won't be able to stop. I would probably kill him too. What a spectacle of violence it would be.

So another day goes by, and I haven't freed Clementine.

As I walk through the forest, it starts to rain. The water comes down in sheets, and my hair sticks to my face in wet chunks. I can't see more than five feet in front of me. My feet squelch with each step, mud oozing up around me.

Tomorrow is my last chance. If I don't do it by then, she'll hang.

I tell myself, foolishly, that perhaps there's a way to rescue Clementine without hurting the guards. Perhaps, inside the lighthouse, there's a key hanging on the wall somewhere, or flimsy hinges I can break. It's only when I convince myself of this—rescue Clementine, don't fight anyone—that I finally, finally get myself unfrozen.

It's deep night. Providence, sleeping, is blacker than the sea, whose inky waves splash stars back at the sky. The guards on their shift are drinking from flasks of something that makes them cough. They're busy laying cards on the dirt, their faces aglow from beneath with flickering lamplight, and it should be hard, sneaking past them, but sneaking past them was never what I was afraid of. Fighting them would take a stomach for violence and a head unfettered by fear, but the sneaking? That only takes one thing, and it's a particular talent of mine.

Being quiet.

The door to the lighthouse creaks when I open it, but I slip through and shut it again before anyone comes to investigate.

Inside, it's cramped. The only light comes from a few flickering candles. And it's *cold*. The wet kind of cold that makes you cough.

The ground floor is round and dominated by stacked barrels. To the left, there's a crumbling staircase. No more guards. And no Clementine. I climb the stairs.

They're made of stone rather than wood, which is, I guess, why they haven't yet fallen apart. As I walk, they rattle and tilt; they're cobbled together with vines pushing up between them.

The second floor must've been where the lighthouse keeper

lived. I don't know what's original and what's been replaced, but it's in even worse condition than the ground floor. It smells like rot. The staircase keeps going—up to the light, presumably—but to the left of the stairs, there's a door frame. The original door must've been ripped out, because now it's just metal bars. Padlocked shut. No key hanging from the wall. No flimsy hinges I can break.

I'll have to fight the guards, then. Hurt them? Kill them? I don't know why I thought it could go any other way.

A shadow shifts behind the bars.

The sound—slow, scratchy—of someone breathing.

I am still and I am silent.

Clementine says, "Thea."

Chapter Twenty-two

THEN

Sixteen years old

Tanager Rock

I ran away with Bauer just before dawn.

The night: sleepless. I spent all of it staring at the ceiling as Clementine's voice echoed through my head.

Thea. Be quiet.

I had a bag packed with spare clothes, but there was one more thing I wanted. Clementine's knife.

If I really wanted to get away with it, I would've slipped straight ashore when everyone was asleep, no detours. But instead, I snuck into Clementine's room.

In the thin light, I navigated by feel, listening to Clementine's easy night-breathing. I rummaged through her desk. A pouch full of coins, jangling when I picked them up. And there were Clementine's knives—she kept four of them in her top drawer. It was one of the most ostentatiously piratical things she did. Four silver knives engraved with her initials. And now, three.

Her breathing got quiet for a minute. I shut the desk drawer loudly, waiting for her to sit up. Say something. That was why I came in here, wasn't it? I didn't need the coins or the knife. I needed to be stopped.

But when I turned, her face was buried in the pillows. She wasn't going to stop me. Hadn't heard me.

I was too good at being quiet.

I crept out of her room.

We didn't often keep prisoners on *Asterope's Revenge*. Clementine said she didn't like wasting the food. So unlike some pirate ships, we didn't have a hold. Commodore Price was being kept in a closet.

The door was locked, poorly—who would try to break him out?—so I picked it with the tip of Clementine's knife. It creaked open, and I saw him inside. The blinking, crumpled heap of a man.

"Get up," I said.

Price was slow to rise. When did he last eat?

"Come on," I said. "Be quiet."

I heard Clementine's voice in my head again. *Be quiet.* I gave Price a shove up the stairs.

On the top deck, someone should've been keeping watch. Benjy. I heard his snores before I saw him. Price and I crossed the deck to the gangway to the dock uninterrupted.

I didn't realize until my feet were on solid ground just how much I'd thought someone would stop me. How much I hoped someone would stop me.

And then what? Clementine would feel bad about how she

treated me? She'd apologize? Clementine had never apologized for a thing in her life.

"Why did you do that?" Price said. His voice was raspy.

"The goodness of my heart," I said. And then I turned to leave.

"Wait!" he said.

"What?"

His eyes flitted across me like there was something on my person that might explain what I'd just done; a little tag tied to my shoe that might say, *Thea Fowler: Frees prisoners in exchange for a warm meal and a good book.*

"What's the catch?" he asked.

People like him, like Clementine, wouldn't ever understand. No catch. What was I getting out of this? Nothing. There was no benefit. Just avoidance. Avoiding my fears. Assuaging my guilt.

"Go," I said quietly. "Before Clementine catches up with you."

Commodore Price turned and ran. And then, with a steadying breath, I did the same.

Bauer was standing on the other side of the harbor, gazing up at the whaling ship. I hadn't expected the smell. It hung in the air, drifted off in waves. Like fish that you'd burned, then left in an outdoor toilet for a week. I put a hand over my face.

"Thea!" Bauer wrapped his arms around me when he spotted me. "I didn't think you'd come."

Neither did I. I pressed my nose into his neck. My lips against his collarbone. I could smell him, just barely, over the whaling ship. His familiar, Tanager Rock smell.

"I'll introduce you to the captain," Bauer said.

The *Pelican* was even bigger than *Asterope's Revenge*—maybe a hundred feet long with a thirty-foot beam. The flag of the Astorian Islands flapped above us, a golden banner with a red trident. The foul smell was strongest at the front of the ship, where big black try pots hulked between me and the wind. I had to fight back vomit.

Bauer marched straight up to the captain, daunted by neither his status nor the smell. But that was Bauer; I'd never seen him daunted by anything.

"Captain Eliot," Bauer said. "This is my friend Thea. You said you had room to take someone else if they knew how to sail?"

The captain looked at me. His skin was a dark bronze color, crinkled around the eyes and dotted with sunspots. "Well, I didn't expect your friend was a girl!" His voice was loud and jovial. "You do know this is a whaling ship, don't you?"

"Yes, sir." Speaking let some of the smell into my mouth. My stomach clenched.

"You ever been aboard a whaler before?"

I shook my head.

"Well, you might soon realize you'd rather sail on a different sort of ship," Eliot said. "But we can give you a try. We've had women sail with us before. Wives and the like. They never last long."

Oh, that word. *Wives*. No to all of it. No, no. "Thank you for the opportunity. I'm—in a hurry to leave."

"A runaway, eh?" Captain Eliot said.

I felt lightheaded at that. Runaway, as a noun. As part of my identity. It wasn't just something I was doing. It was something I was.

"I won't be any trouble," I said.

Eliot considered.

Like with Clementine, like with Benjy, I'd assumed the captain would stop me. Would say I was crazy and send me back to my own ship. Why was it that everyone always told me no—told me I wasn't allowed to do the things I wanted—until now? Until I was doing something entirely too stupid and terrifying to be permitted?

Damn it.

No one was going to stop me. But it scared me more to turn back than to keep going.

We left as the sun was rising. My last glimpse of Tanager Rock was incongruous pastel: lilac clouds and green mosses and soft teal sea. And in that gentle light, *Asterope's Revenge,* her elegant body, her long lines, and someone moving about the upper deck. We were too far away to see who it was.

The wind numbed my fingers, which I wrapped around the railing, and my cheeks, whipped by loose strands of hair.

New settlements. New people. New horizons.

What if I tracked down my grandparents? It'd been years since I'd seen them. What if they were still alive out there somewhere, missing me?

It was hard not to hope. Clementine had always told me I didn't want to be like *normal* girls, *other* girls, but really, I'd never gotten the chance. Maybe I'd be good at coy smiles and ballroom dances. Playing the lyre in the morning light of a sunroom. Sharing a pot of tea with my grandparents while we read.

Now, Grandma Morgan would say, *that's a lovely Clio poem. Read it for us, Thea dear?*

And I would, and Grandpa Morgan would say, *You have a fine voice for poetry.*

I'd thank him, and we'd go back to reading, Grandma Morgan with her poetry, and me with my biology text, and Grandpa Morgan with the newspaper, our silent musings studded by interruptions whenever one of us stumbled upon something that needed sharing.

Maybe I could fill the daughter-shaped hole in their hearts. Maybe they could fill the parent-shaped hole in mine.

I looked back over my shoulder, checking for Bauer. A few of the other sailors were showing him around the rigging, and he was taking to it as easily as he took to everything. The wind carried their voices away, but I could see the ebb and flow of conversation on their faces: Bauer said something charming, and the sailors laughed. The sailors puffed up their chests, sharing some secrets of the trade, and Bauer leaned forward, learning.

The fact that he was here should've made me less, not more, lonely. But there was something about being surrounded by so many strangers that made me feel like he was one of them too, just another sailor I didn't really know.

A hand on my shoulder.

I jumped.

"Whoa, whoa there," Captain Eliot said. "You look awfully serious."

"Oh. Just admiring the view." I tried desperately to catch Bauer's gaze, and like he could hear me thinking, he looked up, started striding across the deck toward me.

"I can't help but notice how familiar you look. Where were you from before Mount Telamon blew?"

Did he know Clementine? My grandparents? *It's just a question. What are you so afraid of?*

"What are you two talking about?" Bauer said. He appeared suddenly, standing in front of me. Protectively.

"Just having a chat with your girl," Eliot said.

His *girl*? I didn't like that. It was like being called a runaway. Not a verb, not an action I could choose to do or not, but a noun. An identity.

Captain Eliot smiled and left us. Bauer stayed, inhaling a deep breath of the sea and the fish smell.

"Isn't it gorgeous out here?" he said.

It was a decent morning. The clouds were scattered and holey. The waves lapped calmly against the hull. We could've done with more wind.

"It's nice," I said.

"I think I'll like life aboard," Bauer said. He gave my hand a squeeze. I pulled back, and he frowned. "What?"

"I just . . ." The other sailors, the ones Bauer was talking to earlier, were watching us, smirking. They were older than us, but not by much. "This is public."

"Too public to hold your hand?" he said. "We got on board together. I don't think it's exactly a shock to anyone that I might hold your hand."

I'd annoyed him. "It's not about whether it shocks them," I said. "I'm just saying that it makes me feel odd."

"Oh, so I embarrass you?" he said. I saw hurt plain on his face, and guilt fissured through me.

He didn't embarrass me. He was one of the best-looking boys I'd ever met, with that strong jaw, that tousled hair. He was charming, and everyone seemed to like him from the moment they met him. Bauer wasn't embarrassing.

Maybe part of me didn't think I belonged with him. Maybe I didn't like the idea that those sailors would say, *Really? Her?* Or maybe I would've felt uncomfortable if any person, no matter how they looked, no matter how they acted, held my hand while others were watching. Maybe it wasn't Bauer; it was the idea of being physically attached to someone.

I was Bauer's girl. That's what Captain Eliot said. Holding his hand made me feel like that. Like my whole identity was belonging with, or to, Bauer.

"Oh, Thea," Bauer said, pitying. "Come here."

He wrapped me in a hug. My body tensed, but I didn't know how to shake him off without hurting his feelings even more than I already had.

A voice echoed across the deck, saving me.

"Spout, ho!"

Bauer's arms dropped, and everyone ran to the port rail and

gazed at the horizon. Spout? I didn't see anything, waterspout or whale.

But if we did—

The smell was suddenly the only thing I could focus on. The smell of rendered blubber.

I should've thought of this the moment Bauer said *whaler*. But I'd been so focused on myself, on my future, that I hadn't spent much time considering the actual logistics of the voyage. The fact that whaling ships kill whales.

Something warm and acidic was rising inside me. Vomit? The last thing I wanted to do was throw up last night's dinner in front of the whalers, so I slipped out of the crowd. They were all still peering at the seascape, searching for the source of that waterspout.

I went to the starboard rail and leaned over it. My lungs sounded wheezy.

Couldn't shoot a killer. Couldn't stomach the thought of dead whales. I really wasn't meant to live on the ocean.

And then, alone on my side of the ship, I saw a body rise from the water.

She was so big, it looked less like she was surfacing and more like the water was receding around her. And then I saw another form, smaller, resting by her head.

A mother and baby humpback. Ten, five feet from me.

The mother's back was slate gray and scarred, her head knobbed with bumps the size of my fist. And pressed against her mouth, her baby's body was limp, back unscarred and head unknobbed. The calf was probably twice my size, but against her mother, she looked tiny. She wasn't moving.

The mother looked up at me—I'm sure she looked up at me. Her eyes were small compared to the rest of her massive body, only the size of my palm. And they were so intelligent I felt like I'd been stripped naked. It wasn't like looking at a bird or a squirrel or a deer, wide eyes that fear you, that watch you like prey watches predator. It was like meeting the eye of a human across a crowded room.

I opened my mouth, but no sound came out.

Her baby never moved.

She was dead, I realized then. The baby was dead, and the mother carried her.

Oh. *Oh,* I wanted to say something, wanted to talk to her, wanted to ask her why and how. Could she see? How awed I was? I'd seen plenty of whales from *Asterope's* deck, but none so close—none that looked me in the eye. The gods had always been myths to me, just stories, but this felt like apotheosis. Like meeting a god.

This animal. This intelligent, compassionate, human creature. Why is it that we judge an animal's intellect by how much emotion they show, but we judge humans by how much emotion they repress?

A dog: smart. It loves me and obeys me and wants to please me.

A butterfly: not smart. Just operating on instinct, flying and mating and dying.

A man: smart. He's stoic and rational.

A woman: not smart. She's commanded by her emotions. Did you see her crying? She's so volatile. She's so unpredictable. She's so hysterical.

I pressed my stomach to the railing.

I see you. Do you see me?

Too soon, the mother whale dipped back below the water's lip, taking her calf with her.

I grabbed for Bauer's arm, but he wasn't there. Of course. He was looking at a different whale, a big, splashing male on the port side of the *Pelican*.

I hurried across the ship to him, pulled him toward me. I didn't want to talk too loudly. I didn't want the rest of the sailors to know about the mother. "I just saw something."

He wasn't looking at me fully; his eyes kept darting toward the male. "The whale?"

"A mother whale," I said. "She had a calf with her, but it was—I don't know how to explain it—it was dead. She was carrying her dead calf with her. It must've died of something, and she was grieving."

Bauer gave me a puzzled smile. "Maybe it was sleeping. Calves probably don't have the same kind of endurance as the adults."

"I know what I saw."

"I'm sure you saw something like that," Bauer said. "But there's a lot you don't know about whales. A lot we both don't know about whales." He added the last bit as though this concession was some kind of olive branch.

"But you didn't see," I said. "Why don't you believe me?"

"You have a brilliant imagination," he said, tucking my hair behind my ear. "I love that about you."

"I saw them," I said. "I did."

But then one of the whalers shouted, and Bauer turned from me.

The breath came out of me in a whoosh of air.

It wasn't just the mother and calf. Wasn't just the big, splashing male.

We were entering a pod bigger than I could've imagined. There were so many sleek backs rising from the water that they could've been rocks in a river, creating their own rapids.

"The whale iron!" someone shouted. "Give it to him, the whale iron!"

I didn't know what a whale iron was until I saw it: a harpoon, spearing the nearest whale through his back.

A few of the men had gotten into a small boat off the side of our ship. This was where the harpoon was attached. It looked too light, too small, to fight a whale. The men were minuscule in comparison. Was that Bauer? No—he was still here, leaning over the railing.

The whale thrashed, slamming his tail against the side of the ship. We rocked precariously. In the water, the other whales, the free ones, circled like sharks. Some fled; others flashed their tails.

The harpooned whale dove. When he disappeared, a coiled line began to spin out wildly. It was attached to the harpoon, I realized. I couldn't imagine that little line holding something as leviathan as the whale. And I didn't want it to.

Get away. Go on. You don't deserve this.

But the line didn't snap. Didn't break or sink the boat. I waited for the whale to run out of breath. It needed air, eventually.

Other men were loading into other boats stacked high with harpoons. I begged the other whales to go, and they did. Swimming hard, keeping their young tucked under their flippers. Diving deep.

When the harpooned whale surfaced again, he rose into an empty, friendless ocean.

He rose into the point of a lance.

The ocean is vast, with plenty of room for blood to dilute and dissipate. But whales, I learned, have an extraordinary amount of blood.

He didn't die quickly, or quietly, or softly, and I made myself watch every minute of it because I felt like I owed him that much. I couldn't give him a longer life or a nobler end, but I could give him the dignity of seeing his death for what it was: an atrocity.

I hunched in the corner of the deck when they hauled him on board. The men from the boat got big congratulations all around; pats on the shoulder, swigs of liquor. It was a humpback, a beautiful humpback, but slumped and deflated on the deck, he didn't look anything like the pictures I'd seen in textbooks.

Then came the disassembly. The sailors didn't spend long admiring their work; they started flensing the blubber and taking it to the try pots to boil and render. I realized that the smell, terrible enough before, was just a week-old remnant of what it could've been. Now it bloomed fully, putrid and piercing.

They cut him apart bit by bit, dispatching him down to his pieces. The fat coating his strong muscles, for oil to power machines and lanterns. The long strips of baleen he used to catch his dinner, unstrung from his mouth to make fishing poles. The bones, which had held his body together when he descended to lightless depths, which made him strong and whole, to be turned into a corset so that some woman, somewhere, might have to hold her breath as she walked down the stairs.

Distantly, I heard Captain Eliot saying that the brute damaged our hull, and we'd need to make repairs. I didn't know whether he told me or someone else. The words passed over me like so much water.

By the time Bauer found me, I'd almost forgotten he was there. The loneliness I felt on that ship was so much bigger than any loneliness I ever felt on *Asterope's Revenge*. There, I was a child among adults; here, I didn't even feel like part of the same species as the sailors. I felt more kinship with the whale. Seeing Bauer, then, was so nonsensical that I just stared at him, blinking. What did this whaler want with me? I belonged underwater; I had to roll my body off the edge of the ship before the harpooners caught me.

"Thea?" Bauer said.

His hands were covered in blood.

"I can't believe what I just saw," he said.

"Neither can I," I said. My mouth was dry. It tasted like metal.

"My parents tried to convince me that I'd be better off running the inn than making my own path, but we're here. We're really here. And I'm finally doing something useful. Did you hear what Captain Eliot said? He said that this was some of the finest baleen he'd seen all year. The lot of it could go for ten gold terns. And I could have one of them, since I was doing so well on my first whale."

A moment of fracture.

I thought of the whale bones we assembled together behind the Tanager Rock Inn. The rib cage we'd so lovingly built. What did I see when I looked at that skeleton? Clues to a creature I wanted to understand. Questions in a scientific puzzle.

What did Bauer see when he looked at that skeleton?

I opened my mouth. Shut it again.

"Thea?" he said. He caught my hand. I tried to shake him away, but he wouldn't let me. "What's wrong?"

You.

"Don't you feel sick?" I said. "Don't you care how brutal that was?"

He pulled me, unwilling, into his arms. This time, he didn't have that familiar, Tanager Rock smell. He smelled only like slaughtered whale.

"I'm sorry you had to see that. I didn't realize. I should've considered your feelings, told you to go below deck."

"That's not it." Didn't he understand? My not going below deck was the only good thing to have happened in the past however many hours. That one moment of courage, of deciding the whale would not die without a friend to mourn him.

"You're scared," he said. "I understand. But we'll be at a settlement soon. You can stay there until we finish the voyage, and then I'll come back for you."

"You don't care," I said. "About the whale."

He gave me a funny look. A confused smile. "Sometimes, I can't believe you were raised by a pirate."

"What? What's that supposed to mean?"

"You're the gentlest girl I ever met." And then he kissed me on the forehead, like a parent would a child. "But Thea. Whales don't have feelings. There's nothing to care about."

"Whales don't have feelings?" I said. Didn't he see the fury and the fear in the whale's eye? Didn't he know there was a mournful mother and her dead calf far below us? Couldn't he believe me when I said I did?

"Thea," he said softly.

He kept saying my name. Like that would prove how well he knew me. But he didn't. And I didn't know him.

"I know you're frightened right now," he said. "But you have no reason to be. Come on. You trust me."

I twisted out of his grasp. I wanted to go somewhere he couldn't see me. Somewhere I couldn't see him or anyone else on this ship. I found the door that led below deck, and I took it, clambering down into a dark, narrow hall. It was lit with flickering lanterns. Probably burning whale oil.

My hands were shaking. I raised them to the light. Oh—Bauer had touched them.

They were stained with blood.

Chapter Twenty-three

Now

Seventeen years old

Providence

"Come here," Clementine says.

I do. I walk toward the bars slowly.

"Clementine?" I say.

Through the bars, the room is dark. There's a window, but it's bricked over. The walls are covered in peeling wallpaper, mustard yellow and streaked with brown-red smudges that look like dried blood. Drawings, I realize. She's drawing plants; stars; animals, just like she did when I was a child. There's no furniture. Just a bucket and a handful of chipped red stones piled in the corners. And then: Clementine.

She drops a chunk of stone, and it clatters to the ground, splitting. Her hair is long and tangled and her clothes are ripped and bloody. Even in here, she looks wild. Lethal.

"I wondered if you were here," she says.

"I'm going to get you out."

We watch each other for a minute, a long minute, and as it unfolds, I realize she knows the truth.

"Commodore Price—" I start.

"You told him about the autumn armistice," Clementine says. "Why?"

I open my mouth. Nothing comes out.

She presses a palm to the bars, tilts her head, assessing. "Why did you leave?"

My throat is too dry for words, so I just shake my head.

"You ran away with that boy from the inn, didn't you? How did you end up here?"

Finally, I manage: "I jumped off a whaling ship."

She inspects me, and I realize I'm holding my breath like a criminal awaiting judgment.

Why do I still crave her approval? Isn't it enough to have survived?

"My own fault, I suppose," she says. "If I'd taught you better, you wouldn't have run away with the first boy who smiled at you."

I feel like I've been kicked in the stomach. The breath goes out of me. It's every time Bauer touched me, every slippery word he whispered in my ear, distilled. Clementine telling me I don't get what she's taught me. Telling me I don't get that men can be bad, that they can hurt you, that they can lie to you.

She means: *You foolish girl.*

She means: *You deserved it.*

"You don't even *know* me," I say, my voice quiet and unsteady. "You never have. You've never even tried. All you care about is having a daughter exactly like you. Exactly like your ridiculous myths about your ridiculous goddesses. The goddess Thea isn't real, Clementine. I'm the only Thea you've got."

She wraps her fingers around one of the bars so tightly her knuckles turn moon white. "You think I don't know the difference between myths and reality? As a little girl, all I wanted was to be so clever that I could make people listen. And then I realized that it didn't matter what I said or how I said it. I was a woman. No one would ever believe me. I wanted to be like Thea from the stories, but I couldn't be. I couldn't do it. So I tried to give you that chance instead."

I open my mouth, but she keeps talking.

"Of course I know you," she says. "I trusted you. I wanted you to captain a ship! If either of us had a mother who didn't know her, didn't trust her, it was me. The only person who ever trusted me was Phin. Do you have any idea how it feels when the only person in the world who trusts you just—" Her words break.

"Do I understand?" I say slowly. "What it means when the only person who trusts you dies? Yes, Clementine. I lost him the same day you did."

I feel like someone has reached inside my guts with a blade and scraped. Hollow; fresh; raw. I feel like someone reached inside of me and ripped everything out.

"You don't trust me," Clementine says.

Her voice echoes. It echoes in dark places inside my head.

Stop it.

It pulls at old memories. And new ones.

Stop.

"Should I?" I say. "Trust you?"

She's quiet. Then: "You jumped off a whaling ship."

"Yes."

"You survived."

"Yes."

I don't like the way she's looking at me—appraising, like she can see through me.

"You hated being a pirate," she says.

"What does that have to do with anything?"

"It doesn't," she says. "Never mind."

We stare at each other for a long moment. Do I trust her? No, yes. Do I love her? Yes, no. Who do I want to be? Her; the goddess Thea; anything but. I'm so tired.

"I'll be back tomorrow night," I say. "With the damn key."

"Thea?" she says as I turn to go. "I love you."

It makes me stop. Still. One foot in the air.

I say nothing in return. I make myself walk again, because what do I do with that? Out the creaky door. I slip between the foolish, incompetent, drunken guards. They would be so easy to kill. It would be simple. Slit a throat, unhook a key from a belt loop. I could do it right now if I wanted to. It's not them that's stopping me. It's me that's stopping me.

They don't even look up from their card game as I creep away from the lighthouse.

The woods shiver around me. Tree to my back, I sink and press my hands to my face.

You don't trust me, Clementine said. I hear her voice like a shout inside a canyon.

You don't trust me.

You don't trust me.

Clementine. Bauer. I don't want to be here. Don't want to be there. Not now; not then. I'm tired of asking myself if I'm crazy. I'm tired of being told—

You trust me.

I don't—

trust

Chapter Twenty-four

THEN

Sixteen years old

Liberan Sea

I stood in the hallway of the bowels of a whaling ship with humpback blood on my hands and time spinning milkily around me. When Bauer found me there, I was still staring at my fingers.

"You're in shock," he said.

It was probably the first true thing he'd said all day.

"Come here," he said, taking my hand, never mind the blood, and guiding me down the hallway.

Distantly, I wondered how he knew his way around. Had he explored before I'd gotten on board? Had some of the other sailors told him? *We saw your girl getting hysterical. Take her to the third door on the left and get her to calm down.*

He led me to what must've been one of the crew bedrooms. There were four cots built into the wall, the kind with ropes knotted in a grid below the wool blankets. Two men were in there, playing cards. They looked up when they saw us. Smirked.

"Hey, greenhand," one of the men said to Bauer.

"Right," Bauer said. "I was hoping we could sit down for a minute."

"Oh, by all means," the man said. "Why don't we go see if Captain Eliot needs any help? We're on break, but maybe it will earn us a few extra petrels." The two men stood. Gave Bauer a smile. It felt like they were communicating in code. Neither of them said anything to me. Neither of them even looked me in the eye.

They left, and Bauer closed the door behind them.

"Come here," Bauer said, sitting on one of the beds.

I hesitated, then followed him. When I sat, it squeaked, and I could feel the knots and gaps of rope through the blankets.

"Hey," Bauer said. "Look at me."

I did. Handsome, charming Bauer. Smiling, whale-flensing Bauer. He tucked my hair behind my ear, brushed it over my shoulder. He was looking at me intently.

"What?" I said.

"You're beautiful," he said. He ran his hands down my neck, my arm, closing around my hand and enveloping it. "Did you know that?"

I'd spent the past three years on a ship, but I'd never been seasick like this before. I felt every slosh of the waves in my stomach. Nausea burned at the back of my throat.

"I don't want to do this," I said, giving him back his hands.

"Thea," he said gently, turning my name into something soft. "You have nothing to be worried about. I know you're scared, but I can protect you."

He kissed me. I started to pull away, but his mouth followed mine.

Because hadn't I always kissed him before? Enthusiastically, even?

"Bauer, don't," I said. Pressure was building behind my eyes. If I cried right now, I wouldn't forgive myself. I had to prove that I was okay. Rational. Thinking logically. Not a ragged, emotional mess from seeing one slaughtered whale.

He looked down at his hands. They were clean. He'd wiped the blood off of them. "I'm so mad at myself. So fucking mad."

Bauer didn't usually curse. I inched a little closer to him again, trying to see his face. His jaw was hard. Lips tight.

"I was being selfish," he said. "I wanted to help you get away from Clementine, and I thought being on this ship together would be—I don't know. Fun? I'm such an idiot."

"I don't—" I wasn't sure how, or when, the conversation had flipped upside down, but I suddenly felt like I was meant to comfort him. Like I was supposed to apologize, even though I wasn't sure what I'd done wrong. "You're not an idiot."

"No," he said, "I am. I should've saved up some money, rented a little ship for just the two of us. We could've sailed away from Clementine by ourselves. Without all of this." He gestured toward the ceiling, above which the whale carcass was slowly getting hacked into discrete bits.

"It's okay," I said, even though it wasn't. He was still looking at his lap. Looking so angry at himself. "Hey," I said, tapping his chin. He turned to me. "It's okay," I said.

He set his hand on my thigh. And then he kissed me again.

It was sudden, surprising, unwanted. The kiss undid the sincerity of everything he'd just said.

It wasn't okay. I'd said it was, *it* being the dead whale, even though it wasn't, even though *I* wasn't.

"This isn't a good idea," I said, shifting to the other end of the bed.

But then he was lying on top of me. An arm on either side of me. Leaning in to kiss me again.

"Someone could come in," I said.

"I locked the door."

"But they could . . . They could unlock it." It wasn't about whether or not the sailors walked in. Maybe it was, a little. It was just one reason out of a hundred that my brain was revolting against this.

Bauer smiled at me, that syrup lazy smile, the playful, flirtatious, easy smile. "We're adults, Thea. We're on our own. Your mother's not watching over your shoulder anymore."

He kissed me hard.

No. This was wrong. I felt like I was moving through the syrup of Bauer's smile. Everything was slow and foggy. He was rationalizing away my protestations before I could even make them. He could win a whole argument without me saying a word.

We'd kissed plenty before, but it had never felt quite like this. With this expectant air of more to come. His body was so heavy. The cot below us squeaked whenever he moved. I don't think I moved. I felt frozen.

"Bauer," I whispered. Something caught in my throat,

blocking the words from coming out right. Were they coming out at all?

He must not have heard me, because he didn't react. He just kept—

"Bauer, I don't—this isn't—"

Kept kissing me.

Kept dragging his hand down my body—neck, chest, hip, thigh—and back up again—thigh, hip, chest, neck—and I didn't understand how I could feel so far away from someone so close to me. Touching so many pieces of my body.

And that's what I was.

I was pieces.

"Leo," I whispered, wondering how long tears had been leaking down my cheeks.

What did I want? I wasn't sure. But not this.

"Come on, Thea," he said. "Don't be like that." He sounded impatient. Sharp. "You trust me."

The hem of my shirt was in his fist, shoved up. Then his hand, bare against my bareness, hot against my cold skin. Stomach, ribs.

I knew, in a distant sort of way, that there was an after to this. There would be a time when the only arms wrapped around me were my own. And then I'd see this moment for what it was and call it what I needed to call it.

But then, I just wanted it to be over.

I closed my eyes. A tear reached the corner of my mouth, and I wondered if Bauer tasted it too.

I was the whale. A body. I was resources, bits and pieces, harvested and taken and dissected. Why is it that when whales sing, no one but me wants to listen? I was a lit lantern and a fishing pole and a woman's corset.

If a girl speaks and no one listens, does she make a sound?

In the silence, over and over again, I heard him saying:

You trust me.

You trust me.

You trust me.

While the rest of the whaler's crew slept in shifts, I lay in the knotted rope bed next to Bauer. It was too small. He sprawled, a leg over my ankles and an arm over my stomach. I stayed very still, pressed against the wall like I could shrink out of existence.

The room had one small window, view obscured by a lacy curtain. Outside, the night was dark, dark, dark.

The more experienced crew members, those more necessary than Bauer, only got a few hours of sleep at a stretch. Dissecting the whale, it seemed, was time-sensitive business. As they changed off, they talked in hushed voices.

"We stopping in Fairshore tomorrow?" one said.

"Should be. Captain Eliot says the repairs will only take a few hours."

And, at the next shift change:

"You reek."

"So do you."

"My girl says I'll always smell like this stuff. Still doesn't stop her when we get shore leave, if you know what I mean."

"Oh, 1 know."

And:

"She's sort of pretty. If you can get over the crazed, wide-eyed thing."

"The crazy ones are always the most fun. The greenhand is smart."

In those small hours, I realized that it was my seventeenth birthday. Seventeen years ago, Clementine had named me Thea and set me loose on the world. What hopes she must've had for her silent little girl. And all it came to was this.

I watched the lacy curtain. The darkness began to ebb, and there it was—the bloom of a new sunrise across a watery horizon.

I could swim.

The idea was so stupid. So crazy. A swim. To where? For what purpose? I was always running, running away, and what good did it do me?

But I stared at the waves, and I considered.

I waited until the shift change was over. Until all the men lay in their beds. Until they were breathing slowly, snoring, limbs splayed like they were untouchable. Like they couldn't imagine not being safe.

Then I stood up. My rucksack was tucked neatly under Bauer's bed. Who'd brought it here? Me? I couldn't remember. All I took was Clementine's knife.

The floorboards creaked under my feet, but I walked lightly. I was surprised I could do that. I felt like the gravity had increased. It was a heavy, sapped sort of grief. Loss. Not of virginity. That, which had been the topic of so many conversations among the boys at Keswick-Fleming, felt absent of meaning. Virginity wasn't what I lost.

This was what I lost:

The picture of the future I'd started painting. A quiet, normal life. Living with my grandparents and waiting at a harbor with bated breath as Bauer came back for shore leave. A version of living where I could be soft and gentle.

The first serious, adult, true love I'd ever felt, or thought I'd felt. This connection born from someone seeing me for me, and me seeing him for him.

The ability to believe myself when I thought: *This is a person worth trusting.*

Would he always be stamped on me? In me?

I'd never understood what it meant to be a girl or what rules I was supposed to follow. *Not like other girls.* That's what Clementine always told me to strive for. But that morning, when everything was still and the light was soft, I was good. I was the thing girls are always told to be.

Leo Bauer, a good boy: a charmer with a too-loud laugh, a son from a humble family who dreamed of making his own way, a brave adventurer who wasn't scared of ships or waves or whales, a hero who saved the girl he loved from her tyrannical mother. And me, a good girl: quiet.

I left without confrontation. I left without a fight. I left with one last look at his face. He was still handsome, still warm, still softly breathing, and I wasn't. My lungs were so tight, and my eyes were wet, but I left, and I didn't make a sound.

He knew I never would. Make a sound. Who would listen? Who would care?

You trust me.

Bauer and I trusted the same things: That I wouldn't scream at him because I didn't know if he was less dangerous than the help that would arrive. That neither of us wanted a narrative about taking and hurting when it was meant to be a love story. That I now felt so disgusted and disgusting that I couldn't imagine burdening someone else with the truth of this.

I didn't know when I became so selfless. Bauer probably knew all along. Expected this of me; of whichever girl he met next. That she would be selfless.

I never trusted Bauer.

But Bauer always trusted me.

CHAPTER TWENTY-FIVE

NOW

SEVENTEEN YEARS OLD

PROVIDENCE

I don't remember falling asleep in the woods, but I must have, because when I open my eyes, I'm not sure what time it is. I'm not even sure what season it is. My head is all full of memory, the line between then and now too thin to see.

It's the day before Clementine's execution.

The rain is still coming down in a steady drizzle. I'm covered in mud, and my wet clothes cling to my body. I stare at it. My body. I rest my head in my palms and just stare, at this body that swims oceans and hikes mountains, at this body that sometimes doesn't feel like mine.

I'm just—

I'm so tired.

Apparently, I fell asleep, but it doesn't feel like it. If anything, I'm more exhausted than I was before. And now, today, I have no more chances, no more hours, no more putting this off:

Today I kill a man.

Throw away everything I've built on my own.

Say goodbye to Providence, and Wes, and his dog, and all those books, forever.

I get to my feet slowly. Stretch. Let myself inhale and exhale, feel the choice settle inside me. I've already made up my mind.

This is just something I have to do.

I walk to the copse of trees with the best view of Providence's harbor. The spectacle of violence is in full swing: dozens of unfamiliar faces; a few men playing fiddles; families peddling wares from tents and the backs of carts. The lively trade Commodore Price always wanted finally seems to be starting. It smells like fires and baking bread.

A dog barks. I spot Clipper. Wes is close behind him, and Di. They're both holding cups of something, and they look vaguely concerned. But then Wes smiles—just a little—and it's enough to turn me to stone.

The spectacle of violence. His words. And it's all a big party. A festival.

I hope he has fun.

Clipper turns his head and barks directly at me. Wes's eyes follow. *Move.* Not quick enough. He sees me, and the smile vanishes. Di looks too, and her concerned expression deepens.

What do they see when they look at me? Wild, unbelonging girl. Crazy, matted, hollow-eyed girl. It doesn't matter. After tonight, I'll never see them again.

I turn and leave the festival behind me. I'm not hungry anymore.

. . .

I get back to the lighthouse to resume my vigil just as the sun is setting. That worries me. I would've guessed it wasn't much past noon; I must've slept much, much longer than I thought.

At first, everything looks normal. The rough, white stone of the lighthouse is turned pink and yellow with the faint colors of a cloudy sunset; the grass around it is misted and green. In the background, the waves crash and echo against the cliffs.

And then I see the dead body.

His limbs are splayed out, starfish-like, by the door. A guard. There's a crater in the side of his head, all blood and bits, and I know I should honor him and the atrocity done to him, but I can't think past my revulsion.

You were going to kill someone. Him, maybe.

I stumble toward the lighthouse. One foot trips the other. I catch myself on the rough facade of the outer wall, scraping my palms. But it holds me up.

Slowly, carefully, I walk inside.

The door creaks loudly, and this time, I push it all the way, let the hinges squeal.

"Hello?"

No answer.

I take the stairs slowly, trying to make up for the humming-bird pace of my heart.

"Clementine?"

The door of her cell hangs open.

Empty.

I step inside.

What *happened?* Did Livia and Cadmus already show up? Did Clementine think of a way to get herself out?

Oh—

"She left me," I say.

She left me here.

I touch my hands to my face, feeling my cheekbones, my jaw, the shape of a face that has never looked enough like Clementine's. And then I see, through the openings in my fingers, the scrawl of her messy handwriting. The words in red.

All across the wall, pictures. Cypress trees and humpback whales and long-fingered hands. The rusty markings of oxidized rock turned beautiful by her artist's touch. In front of me, each letter as big as my palm, a sentence:

You are Asterope's revenge.

PART FOUR

THE MYTH OF ASTEROPE

THEN AND NOW AND THEN

Then and now and then, there was a girl named Asterope.

She was the daughter of gentle Aris, a prophet of the sea god Saleus. Aris had six daughters, but Asterope was the most beautiful, with a high, clear singing voice that made all who heard her stop to listen.

One sunrise, while Asterope bathed in a secluded lagoon, hotheaded Saleus heard her singing. He traveled from the other end of the ocean to find the source of the song, and when he arrived, he was smitten by bright-eyed Asterope's mortal beauty. He rose from the waves to claim her. Asterope, startled, fled.

Saleus was angry that Asterope had not kneeled before him. He found her father, Aris, praying at his seaside altar.

"Tell me your daughter's name," the sea god Saleus said.

"I have many daughters," Aris said.

"The most beautiful one," Saleus said. "The one who sings like a siren."

Asterope was brought in front of Saleus.

"She ran from me," Saleus said. "She will apologize."

"I'm sorry," Asterope said.

"Liar!" Saleus said. "You feel no remorse."

Indeed, Asterope wasn't sorry. Hotheaded Saleus frightened her. She yearned to flee again, but she worried Saleus might take out his ire on her father. She stood before the god with her head hung.

"Your daughter disrespects me," Saleus told Aris, "and she does not speak the truth. You will sacrifice her to me at sundown."

Gentle Aris shook his head. "I cannot."

"You dare love your daughter more than me?" Saleus boomed.

"I do," Aris said, ashamed.

"You both spurn me," Saleus said. "So I will punish you both. I curse you, Asterope. For the rest of your days, you will always speak the truth, and no man will ever believe you."

He vanished into the waves.

Aris knew now that he would never arrange a marriage for his most beautiful daughter—or perhaps any of his daughters. No man would agree to bear Saleus's wrath.

Word spread of Asterope's curse. Aris's daughters, once objects of great desire to kings and warriors alike, were now treated with suspicion. Heroes with brave hearts and firm minds sought out bright-eyed Asterope, believing they alone could see past her curse. But every prophetic word she spoke to them was met with distrust. No matter how many of Asterope's truths came to pass, no man would ever believe her.

A year after Asterope was cursed, her land was gripped with

mourning and celebration: The king had died, but his eldest son, a handsome war hero, was to be coronated. The prince claimed his father had died of a stopping of the heart, but Asterope knew otherwise, and she felt a duty to share the truth.

She walked for one day and one night to the palace. There, she climbed atop a pedestal and spoke to the crowd below.

"Our king did not die," Asterope said. "The prince laced his wine with the venom of the sea dragon so that he could take the throne." She knew what she spoke was true; she had not spoken anything but fact in a year.

"She lies!" the prince said.

"She lies," the people agreed.

The prince was coronated. His first order was to have slanderous Asterope executed. She was taken to the highest balcony of the palace, which overlooked the wrathful sea below. The prince, now the king, ordered her bound in chains. She was tossed off the balcony and into the ocean.

Hotheaded Saleus was eager to finally have his sacrifice. But as he searched for her sinking body, someone else searched faster.

Baelenes, king of the whales, had been watching bright-eyed Asterope's brave admission. He watched the cruel king's men put her in chains. And when she landed in the sea, he found her and broke her free.

"You showed great courage, speaking the truth about your king," Baelenes said.

"You knew I spoke the truth?" Asterope asked.

"Of course," Baelenes said.

Saleus never found Asterope. Baelenes and Asterope together were too clever a team. They married and lived peacefully for the rest of their days. What Asterope spoke to Baelenes was always true, and he always believed her, for he was no man.

Asterope feared she would pass her curse to her children. But when their first daughter arrived, Asterope and Baelenes were overjoyed to realize that only half of Saleus's wrath lingered. Their daughter, whom they named Melia, spoke only the truth, like her mother. But from her father, she had inherited trust and trustworthiness. When Melia spoke, all creatures of sea and land listened, and all creatures of sea and land believed.

Chapter Twenty-six

Now

Seventeen years old

Providence

I sit back on my heels and touch a hand to my throat.

I want, so much, to be believed.

I want, so much, to be loved.

Slowly, I shut my eyes. What a stupid thing to think. What a stupid thing *not* to think.

When Clementine read the myths, the story of Asterope called out to her so much, she named her ship after it. Why this one? Of course this one.

So many of the myths are stories of men. They move in straight lines: Hero goes on quest; hero defeats great villain; hero returns; hero is loved. And then there are these stories, women's stories, that don't seem to start or end in quite the right place, that seem to move in circles, that are over right when you feel like perhaps they've just begun. Asterope never gets to defeat her villain. She never gets to avenge the man who cursed her, or break her curse, or even prove to the people of her kingdom that she never lied about the king. She doesn't get to go back to her family. She never gets to walk on dry land again.

But Asterope gets to survive.

Someone hears, listens to, believes Asterope.

Someone loves Asterope.

This is a story about women and girls.

This is a story about being believed.

How many times was Clementine not believed? When she said she wanted to study. When she said she wanted to attend university. When she said we would die if we didn't listen, and we didn't. I have this picture of her in my head, this woman whose ferocity was absolute. She knew it made her more vulnerable to fall in love. But still, she loved my father. She knew people didn't believe her. Didn't hear her. She knew if she had a daughter, people might not believe her, either. But she dared anyway.

This, I realize, was Asterope's revenge: Knowing the world can be cold and cruel, and choosing to love someone anyway. Knowing the world did not believe you, but hoping it believes your daughter.

Outside, the wind howls.

She left. She left me. Not because she wanted to abandon me, but because for the first time, she believed I could survive on my own. She thought I could be—happy?

I think I hear voices in the distance. Clementine?

The cobbled stairs clatter as I run down them. When I see the dead guard again, my stomach stops while the rest of my body keeps going. For a minute, I'd tricked myself into thinking that Clementine and I were one and the same, but the body. The murder. How can she be so many things? How can she be so awful? How can I still want to say goodbye to her?

At the edge of the cliff, I cup my hands over my eyes and search the horizon. The rain hitting the water bounces back up, obscuring the line between sea and sky in a haze of gray. But then I spot it: the faint golden glow of a ship with lights lit. *Lady Melia*. Livia's ship. I don't see any rowboats struggling toward it or from it, but that doesn't mean they're not there.

I start to turn.

Crack!

A blast fractures the air. A gun going off.

I feel the wind around me, a dart of energy past my forearm. It's already passed and I'm still tipping back, angling away from where it was.

My stomach lurches.

I feel like I'm walking down a staircase and I've missed the last step—that moment when everything feels weightless, then, *thud,* a heavy foot on solid ground. I'm waiting for a *thud* that doesn't come.

Falling.

The world speeds. To my left, the cliff rushes upward, a blur of stone and tufts of grass I can't grab. Everywhere else, there's just air, empty, open. And below me, careening closer, the ocean.

I gasp for air.

Then I crash into the waves.

Chapter Twenty-seven

NOW

Seventeen years old

Liberan Sea

Everything's black.

I kick toward the surface. There is no surface. I try to grab something, anything, but my hands just close around water.

The salt burns my eyes, but I keep them open, searching for something like light. I surge forward, thinking it's air, but it's not the right color. The darkness gives way to that faint, turquoise glow of tiny, living things. Through the murk, I can make out a long tangle of kelp, just one, but I can't tell if it's growing up or down.

My head aches from the pressure. How deep am I? Too deep for a person. Too deep to survive.

A current catches hold of me and yanks me sideways. I open my eyes against the burn of salt, and I'm face-to-face with a whale.

Two whales, actually. I just see the small one at first: a calf, eyes closed. Then, behind her, a massive mother humpback, the largest creature I've ever seen.

Are you real? I want to ask. Are you real, or am I dying, drowning, caught in a web of memory as the real world slips out of reach?

A mother and a calf. The calf isn't moving.

She's not the same whale I saw two months ago. This isn't the same calf. Right? That's not possible. I must be—dying.

The calf is dead already; the mother is watching me.

Is something true if you're the only one who believes it?

I'm not even sure I believe it.

An invisible current tugs me, pulling me farther into the darkness. I reach out, scrabble at nothing.

The mother whale dives. With her nose, she gives the calf's body a gentle nudge; there the baby goes: drifting into the dark abyss. Mother whale swims toward me.

I wait for her to fill her mouth with water, to bare her baleen for me to see. I wait for a crash of her leviathan body or a slap of her powerful flippers. I wait for her to show me how strong she is.

She stops short of touching me, like maybe she's inspecting, considering.

I've heard stories of whales saving humans before. From sharks and storms. And it's almost too much to fathom, that they would show us that sort of kindness when all we do is slaughter them. Scholars are so resolutely baffled at this sort of story. It's the kind of story they dismiss with a laugh, calling the storytellers liars, because it's just too impossible to conceive of a logical, rational reason why a whale would save a person.

Like it's too impossible to conceive of a reason why a whale would grieve. Or why a whale might say goodbye to her calf, finally, because there's another drifting child whose life could still be saved.

Her eye meets mine. Everything burns, my skin and my lungs and my throat, but I can't look away.

She lets out a long, resonant noise. Around me, the amniotic ocean swirls.

And then the whale nestles against me. She touches her vast flipper to my skin, holding me the way a mother would hold a baby, the way she would hold a live calf. She's the strongest being who's ever touched me, but the touch is as light as seaweed.

To her, I'm no bigger than a flipper. To her, I'm another human who wants to see her slaughtered.

And yet.

I reach out so carefully, hoping my fingers are as gentle as her flipper. I rest my palm against her side.

We're made of the same stuff. The same questions: *What do you know? What do I know?* The answer feels as vast as the whole sea and as small as my two hands cupped together, holding the salt and the bacteria and the sound of the ocean. Her song is thin and clear. She sings as if to say, *I will show you strength in the gentlest touch.* And I exhale bubbles, asking everything. *Listen,* she says. *Listen.*

Water eddies around us.

I've forgotten that to survive, I need to breathe.

She takes one enormous stroke.

And above me, I see light.

. . .

My head breaks the surface.

I gasp and blink away the salt. My lungs and eyes burn. I duck under the water again, searching for the whale, but she's gone. She's so entirely gone that I'm half convinced I dreamed her. My skin tingles where she touched it.

I'm about thirty feet from the cliff's edge, but the water is deep-dark below me. From down here, I can't see *Lady Melia* anymore, and I can only just make out the sandy beach.

A wave pulls me farther back. I try to dive beneath it, but I'm not fast enough. My sinuses fill with salt. I flail for the surface just in time to get smacked in the face with another wave.

"Thea!"

The voice skitters across the water. I spin.

"Thea," Wes calls again, and this time, I see the shape of him, the shape of a rowboat fighting its way toward me.

"What are you doing?" I call back.

"Helping," he says. "You owe me a thousand jars of honey."

I paddle to the rowboat. When I reach it, Wes grabs my hands and hauls me up. We nearly capsize. The boat tips left, tips right, then steadies.

"I really appreciate your dedication to athletics," he says, "but now hardly seems like the time for a swim."

"Again," I say, "*what* are you doing?"

He stares back at me. He's as soaked as I am, hair and clothes and leather cord on his wrist. Water clings to his long eyelashes. "I saw you from the harbor, and I tried to come find you. I looked all over the forest. And then I heard voices, so I came to the cliffs. I saw you fall."

"From the lighthouse," I say.

"And I was pretty sure you were dead, so please excuse my eyes, which are red entirely because of the saltwater."

"Why didn't you leave?" I say.

"Why would I leave?"

"Because of what I said. About your father. That I should've killed him."

"Did you kill my father?" Wes asks.

"No," I say, "but what if I did? You were so mad at me."

"So, there's a difference—and it's subtle, but stay with me— between being mad at someone and being willing to let them die."

"Speaking of which," I say, "I have to go find Clementine."

"*We* have to go find Clementine," he says. "We're a team."

"You are incredibly aggravating," I say.

"I'm aware."

We start rowing.

My brain is slow to remember why I fell off the cliff's edge in the first place—a gunshot. Pirate or Providence sailor? There was so much rain; whoever had the gun might not have recognized me. Then again, maybe they knew exactly who I was and shot anyway.

Clementine might've made it as far as *Lady Melia,* but Wes would've spotted another rowboat if it passed. Which means Clementine is probably still on shore somewhere.

"I still can't believe you didn't leave," I say.

"Well, I didn't," Wes says. "What I lack in self-preservation, I make up for in loyalty."

We row, row, row.

"But *why*?" I say.

Wes sets down the oars and opens his arms.

I hesitate. "Is this going to be sentimental?"

"Yes," Wes says.

I hug him, and it is sentimental, but it's not the worst.

He rests his chin on top of my head and says, "I love you, idiot."

When we reach the shore, I say, "What happened at the light-house?"

"What do you mean?" Wes asks.

"One of the sailors was . . . someone killed him."

Wes shakes his head. "I didn't see. I have no idea."

"Where do—" I start.

Bang.

"What was that?" Wes says.

It sounded like a gun. We both already know that.

We run.

My heart pounds too fast in my chest. Clementine, Clementine, *Clementine.*

I stop. Wes freezes beside me.

On the watery stretch of beach in front of us, Clementine

and Commodore Price face each other. Both of their guns are out. Commodore Price's forearm is bleeding: a big red poppy, flowering across his sleeve.

Oh, Clementine. What have you done?

Bang.

Clementine falls.

Her body crumples on the sand.

I run to her. Wes runs too, but not to Clementine. He runs past me, but I can't move beyond her, can't move at all, because now I'm on the ground, collapsed beside her.

"Clementine," I say. "Shit, you're fine. *Shit shit shit.* You're fine. Look at me. Clementine? Mom?"

She's not fine. The wound is through her torso. I don't know what it hit, heart or stomach or lungs, but it's in that central region of important organs, and the blood is weeping out of her.

There's so much blood. Maybe because we're sitting in water, water that's rushing forward and swirling around us and turning all the sand pink. Maybe it's because I've never seen a whole human body's worth of blood rush out of someone before.

She's not fine.

I grip her hands tightly, and she doesn't grip half as hard in return.

"Hey," I say, squeezing. "Clementine."

"Thea," she says.

I have to say something, have to say everything, right now, because what other chance will I have? I'm drowning in the urgency of it. In this last, terrible moment, I want to tell her that I miss my father like a lung, and I know she does too. I want to tell her that I wanted to be her, stoic and unflinching. You could be so cruel, Clementine, and that's never going to be okay, but you also taught me so much about strength and courage and cleverness, and most of all, you taught me how to teach myself. I will never be a mythical hero—not Thea, not Asterope, not Melia—but I'm me, I'm a real person, and isn't that better? I can fail and grow and change.

"I love you," I say instead. It's what I have time for.

"I love you," she says. "Brave, clever . . ." She squeezes her eyes shut, and I wait, breathless, for her to finish.

Wait. Wait . . . Say her name over and over again. She coughs, eyes open again—and I know she sees me—but all too soon, she doesn't, doesn't see me anymore, doesn't see anything anymore.

She's not moving.

She's not breathing.

"No, no, no," I whisper, trying to do something with the blood staining the sand around me.

From far away, I hear Wes shout. I look up.

Commodore Price's gun is raised, and it's pointed at me.

Wes slams against him.

Commodore Price is bigger, but he wasn't expecting that. Wes grabs the gun and backpedals, holding it out of his father's reach, and when Commodore Price looks at me, I see hatred and fear, and I feel myself go cold.

Clementine's gun is in the sand beside her. I take it. Slippery and hot with blood. I flip off the safety and raise it.

Commodore Price's eyes widen.

Shoot him. I won't always be around to protect you. If something happens to me, you're facing the world alone. You want to be a captain? Prove that you're strong enough.

Shoot him.

My finger fidgets with the trigger.

"Thea," Wes whispers.

"You wouldn't," Commodore Price says. The blood keeps streaming down his arm. "You wouldn't shoot."

But I can see in his eyes that he doesn't believe it.

He shot Clementine. She was right here, just a minute ago, and now she's not, now she's gone—

But then: *Flash,* memories rushing, and I'm thinking of a mother whale touching me. Impossibly gentle in her strength. And *flash, flash,* I'm thinking of Wes telling me he loved me, idiot. And *flash, flash, flash,* I'm thinking of Clementine looking at me like we were made of the same stuff, and that stuff was good and strong even if we didn't understand it entirely.

The gun is shaking, heavy in my hands.

I only have a moment to decide: Would I rather Commodore Price die thinking I am strong, or would I rather live knowing that I am? His definition or mine. They're mutually exclusive.

I am finished choosing men over myself.

When I lower the gun, it's not for him. It's not even for Wes. It's for me.

Something in Commodore Price's expression shifts when I drop the gun to the sand. It's not triumph. Not victory. It's *shame*. I see it in the tightening of his lips, the curling of his shoulders. He sailed across a moral horizon I wouldn't cross. He and Clementine, neither of them were ever afraid to pull triggers because in their heads, that's the way the world works, would always work. And now, I break a cycle.

He takes a step backward, pressing a hand to his arm. "Wes," he says. "Come on."

"Oh, fuck you," Wes says.

I love him, the idiot, so much.

"*Wes,*" Commodore Price snaps.

"Get someone else to stitch up your arm," Wes says.

"She would've killed me if I hadn't," Commodore Price says. "She was a *pirate*."

A father searches for something in a son's face and doesn't seem to find it.

In his own way, Commodore Price has always loved Wes, I think. Even if he's never been good at communicating it. Even if he's never been able to fully see Wes for who he is. And I can tell that the expression on Wes's face is breaking Commodore Price more than my bullet ever could have.

Commodore Price looks like he wants to say something more. But instead, he just turns. Then he's gone, and Wes is throwing his gun in the ocean and coming across the pink sand toward me. Me, and Clementine's body.

I drop the gun and take hold of her shoulders. I still think it's a scheme, don't I? Part of some elaborate trick? Because Clementine is invincible. She's too brave. Too clever. Too strong.

"Clementine?" I whisper; my voice can't go any louder. I lace her cold fingers in mine.

And then it hits me, really, actually, that she's not about to open her eyes.

I fall into her, my breaths ricocheting faster and faster and giving me no air.

"Thea," Wes says beside me.

I break.

This is how I break.

My breathing, so fast only a moment before, stops entirely, like cotton is wedged in my throat. I do not breathe, and I do not breathe, and I do not breathe.

I fold in half, and I don't breathe; I scream. I'm not sure whether any noise comes out.

"Clementine," I say to her, gripping her hand with all my wavering strength. "I love you."

And in the end, that's all that's left.

In the end, it's just me; just me, just the love so enormously vast in my stomach, like oceans, uncontainable.

Chapter Twenty-eight

Now

Seventeen years old

Providence

I'm still sitting on the beach with Clementine's body when the sun rises. I always thought morning horizons were the best part of sailing—a refreshing, a newness; but today doesn't feel fresh or new. Today feels achy and cold, and I am heavy with grief.

Wes sits beside me and leans his shoulder against mine.

That's how Livia finds us. A group of pirates row to shore when the storm passes. I hear their voices carried across the waves before they land. It takes them so long that they've already figured out the scene, the body in my arms, and begun grieving.

Livia drops to her knees on the other side of Clementine. The other pirates stand in a loose circle around us. There's no moment of reunion. Not now; not with Clementine—

"What happened?" Livia asks, her voice tight.

I am so, so tired.

"A stand-off," I say. My throat is raw and my voice creaks. "She shot Commodore Price. Then he aimed better."

Livia narrows her eyes at Wes, no doubt tallying the similarities in appearance between him and his father, but I say, "Leave it, Livia. He's fine."

"You got her out of the lighthouse, then?" Livia asks.

"What? No. I thought you did."

Livia shakes her head. "By the time we got here and figured out where they were keeping her, the guard was dead and she was gone. We couldn't find her, so we figured she'd spotted *Lady Melia* and gone that way. But when we got back to the ship, no one had seen her."

"Well, it wasn't me," I say. "She was already gone when I showed up."

"So she got herself out," Livia says, admiring.

"Why am I not surprised?"

We're both quiet for a minute.

"What now, then?" Livia asks.

"I don't know."

"Well . . ." Livia says. "That's it, then. She's really gone."

"Yes."

Livia and I both look at Clementine's cold, pale face.

"Come with us," Livia says. "On *Lady Melia*. It's what Clementine would have wanted."

"No," I say. "I don't think so."

Livia opens her mouth like she's going to protest, but in the end, she just shakes her head. "Okay." A pause. "Can we bury her at sea?"

"She'd like that," I say.

"I think so."

Livia and I carry her body to the rowboats, lifting her gently inside one of them. I stay there for a long time, not willing to let go of her arms, knowing that once I do, she's really gone. But eventually, I do, and eventually, she is.

"Do you think you'll come back?" I ask Livia, leaning against her.

She leans back. It's not quite a hug, but it's not quite not a hug either. "If that's okay."

"I'll write to you at Tanager Rock," I say. "We can figure something out."

"It's just goodbye for now. Until next time."

And there will be a next time. I know that as well as I know anything. In the book of myths, this is what I learned: No endings. Tidy conclusions are always hiding something. The tidier, the more they're hiding.

Wes and I stay there on the beach, listening to the waves, as Livia and the others row back to *Lady Melia*. We watch as they light Clementine's rowboat. We watch until smoke clouds the air and the pyre sinks, and I imagine that somewhere far below, a mother whale is taking care of her.

When *Lady Melia* is a mote on the horizon, Wes says, "How are you?"

"Do you think your father will arrest me?"

"For what?"

"Almost freeing Clementine. Almost shooting him."

"But you didn't," Wes says.

"I gave it some serious thought."

"No," Wes says, "he won't arrest you. If you want to stay here, in Providence, you can. I'll make sure you can. If you want to."

I roll the possibility over in my mind.

"Just because I didn't kill your father doesn't mean I want to see him every day."

"Fair enough. I don't want to see him most days, either."

I tuck my knees to my chest and stare at the water. The lack of Clementine sits in my body like a physical thing—a little in my heart and a lot in my lungs. I'm not just processing the loss of her but the loss of myself. Who am I if not a reaction to Clementine? The foggy chasm of aimlessness gapes before me.

I consider the lessons of Asterope: Tell truth loudly, even if no one wants to listen. Surround yourself with people who believe you. Make the world better for the voices that speak after yours.

As I tell Wes my plan, he listens.

"Think I can do it?" I ask.

"Of course," he says. "When have I ever not believed in you?"

Chapter Twenty-nine

Now

Seventeen years old

Galatean Mountains, east of Providence

When I set off into the mountains, I'm armed with artifacts of kindness—dried goat jerky from Di and hand-me-down boots from Hanna and three crisp, leather-bound notebooks from Wes. As I go, I draw maps, though I'm not as good as my father, and sketch plants, though I'm not as good as Clementine.

It doesn't feel like the last time I went up the mountains. This time, I know I'm coming back.

On the way through Takvik, I buy a loaf of bread.

"Got any more honey?" the baker asks.

"Not right now," I say.

"I like your haircut, by the way."

I accept the loaf of bread, hot through its paper. I look him right in the eye and say, "Thank you."

Not just for this loaf of bread.

It takes me two weeks to reach the first of the river towns. On the fourteenth day, I spot it—a wooden city in the base of a valley, rowboats dotting the water. The autumn colors are raucous. I sit down on the trail and try to capture the scene, but with my pencil, there's no replicating the larches and aspens, the yellow-and-red blaze that glows like the last flames of a funeral pyre.

The town smells like cooking fires and spices. It takes me a while to find someone who speaks Astorian, but I finally do. She's not much older than me, but she carries herself with the air of someone in charge. Her hair is the color of wet sand, and she wears it braided in a crown around her head.

I think of the way I felt the first time I saw Hanna. That surge of hope that she was alone, a tradeswoman, independent, and that if she could be those things, so could I. And now—I hope again.

When I tell her what I'm after, she gets a smile at the edge of her lips.

"I think I can help with that," she says.

She guides me to one of the wooden buildings and into a stone-floored chamber. There, protected from the elements, are shelves upon shelves of books.

I sink to my knees in front of them and touch the spines. *A Surgeon's Guide to Anatomy. Cetology. On the Health of Women.*

My chest feels full, full of sentimental sunrise light. This is what I came here for.

Once, my parents told me I would be a scientist. That I would study the same things men study, and I would do it better than them. But I'm not interested in studying what they study, and I'm not interested in competing with anyone.

"Copy them, if you'd like," the woman says. "There's a good one on botanical medicine. That's the reason I made one of the Astorians who lives here teach me your language."

"We have a few others in Providence," I say. "None as good as this. But I can bring them back, if you'd like."

"Well then," she says. "I suppose we'll have to be friends."

I realize I'm waiting for something to go wrong. Time passes, interim days and interim months, in patterns that become familiar. Too familiar? Too easy? Eventually, I conclude that this is just life doing what it does—going on. I set off again and again with my bag full of empty notebooks and Clementine's knife on my hip. I wear holes in my boots. I fill pages. When I visit a place, I ask for its science, and I ask for its stories. I listen.

Wherever I go, I go to the water. River cities and lake cities and especially ocean cities. I strip off my boots and my muddy clothes; leave them in a pile with my books. When I dunk my head, the world comes up sparkling through wet eyelashes: cypress boughs covered in diamonds; birds tilting their wings and skimming a dazzling horizon.

I find plenty of places I like, but I love Providence best. Colder days chase away autumn, and on the first morning of the new year, it's so cold in my cottage that I linger in bed a long time. I move quietly, gathering my notebooks and my sweater. I have to step over Wes's shoes, positioned tidily by the door, and his sleeping dog, sprawled considerably less tidily, and then I'm outside, breathing crisp air. I make my way to my favorite rocky tidepools and leave my notebooks and shoes stacked on a bit of dry grass.

Behind me, up on the cliffs, the trees make the wind smell sweet and citrusy, and most of their white flowers have already turned to fruit. How long did I crouch among those trees, not recognizing them? I've heard them referred to as winter miracles, and now I understand why. The species seems too obvious to bear mention.

It's early, and the sun is just rising above the vastness of ocean. I pick my way across the tide pools until I'm standing in the belly of it, the sea, toes curling in cold water and mouth full of salt air.

I stare out at the water, breathing in time with the movement of the waves.

Softly, to myself, I say, "She's calm today."

Softly, the ocean whispers something in return.

Sailors call the ocean She. Beautiful She and tempestuous She and emotional She. Maybe they call the ocean She because they want to pretend they can control her, the way men have so often controlled women. Or tried to. Maybe, when they look out on this unpredictable vastness, they want to convince themselves they are more than a speck.

When I dunk my head in the water, the cold shocks me. I come up gasping.

The ocean doesn't care what we want her to be—warm sailing weather or quiet winds. She can be glassy waves. She can be a tempest.

I will be a She like the ocean.

Are you listening? She whispers. *I'm going to tell you a story.*

I believe her.

ACKNOWLEDGMENTS

When I wrote my first book, *Girls at the Edge of the World*, I thought, "That was very personal. Too personal. I won't do such a thing again." And yet, here we are.

Writing Thea's story was both challenging and cathartic. I'm so damn grateful I got the chance to do it.

All my thanks to the people who helped this book come to be, but especially to my agent, Danielle Burby, and my editor, Ellen Cormier. I wrote about ten different versions of this book, and both of you read and reread them. Danielle—I'm endlessly grateful for your optimism, patience, and knack for knowing what I'm trying to say even when I'm not getting the words right. Ellen—this book is so much better because you helped me trust the heart of it.

Thank you to Lauri Hornik and Nancy Mercado for making Dial such a great home for my books. Many thanks also to Cerise Steel for the incredible interior design, Kaitlin Yang for the stunning cover, and Regina Castillo for her copy editing expertise. I'm very grateful to Jennifer Dee, my publicist, and the wonderful marketing team: Felicity Vallence, Shannon Spann, James Akinaka, Christina Colangelo, Bri Lockhart, and everyone else who has helped spread the word about my books.

Thank you also to Debra Polansky and the Penguin Young Readers sales team. And of course, a massive thank-you to everyone who read *Girls at the Edge of the World*.

Huge thanks to my writer friends, and especially to Rosaria Munda, Rachel Morris, Allison Saft, and Ava Reid for fielding my frantic publishing questions. I don't know how I'd muddle through this strange industry without you.

Many hugs and thanks to all my family and friends who stuck by me while I was writing this book, even when I got cranky. Special thanks to Ariana for a million messages across the Pacific. Thank you to the Biggars, the Kitchen Toad crew, and my Melbourne triathlon friends, who helped me fall in love with Australia. Especially massive thanks go to Oliver, master of plot math and generous reader of outlines. And thank you, always, to Aidan, whose kindness, steadiness, and resilience bring me joy every day—yipou're mipy bipest fripiend.

Finally, thanks to Mom, Dad, and Drew. For everything else.